ONE SWORD LESS

Working on a defence project in a research laboratory, electronic engineer Richard Brendon discovers that he has become part of the cold war. Agonisingly, Brendon is required to balance the lives of his wife and children against co-operation with a foreign power. Forced to use his technical expertise to further a plan to precipitate nuclear war, he takes desperate action to prevent the project and save millions of people from certain destruction.

COLIN D. PEEL

ONE SWORD LESS

Complete and Unabridged

LINFORD
Leicester

First published in Great Britain by
Robert Hale Limited
London

First Linford Edition
published 2005
by arrangement with
Robert Hale Limited
London

British Library CIP Data

Peel, Colin D.
    One sword less.—Large print ed.—
Linford mystery library
    1. Detective and mystery stories
    2. Large type books
    I. Title
    823.9'14 [F]

    ISBN 1–84617–074–5

Published by
F. A. Thorpe (Publishing)
Anstey, Leicestershire

Set by Words & Graphics Ltd.
Anstey, Leicestershire
Printed and bound in Great Britain by
T. J. International Ltd., Padstow, Cornwall

This book is printed on acid-free paper

And there went out another horse that was red: and power was given to him that sat thereon to take peace from the earth, and that they should kill one another: and there was given unto him a great sword.

Revelation 6

1

The fragile eggshell of peace lies delicately over the world, intact but for a few small ruptured areas where pockets of local war rage sporadically on the surface below.

A casual observer could be forgiven for concluding that global peace is within the reach of man at last — and so it may be. But the calm is deceptive. A close inspection will show how very precarious is the precious shell and how critical the balance of pressures and stress that maintain its almost unbroken continuity.

The ingenuity of man flourishes in an unprecedented frenzy of activity as he strains to out-think, out-guess and out-manoeuvre his enemies at the deadly game he calls the cold war. Never in the history of Earth have such enormous resources been deployed in the development of weapons of such massive destruction capability.

In order to prevent the outbreak of international conflict of unthinkable proportions, the nations of the world arm and re-arm in a whirling spiral from which, at present, escape is quite impossible.

The environment is such that a small mistake can not only lay open the defence of a nation or alliance, but bring total destruction of our civilisation one dangerous step nearer. It is for this reason that extreme caution must be exercised in all matters of national security and military importance.

On August 23rd 1973, the Department of Defense of the United States of America made a mistake. A stupid, trivial and small mistake, but a mistake nevertheless. One of sufficient magnitude to alert the defence ministries of five major nations and cause me to leave my office in Bristol to attend a special meeting in London.

As Project Leader of the radar system for the terrain-following low-level attack aircraft PN49, I had been invited, or rather instructed, to make my way to the outskirts of the capital in time for briefing of the afternoon of August 26th. I had been told only that the United States had accidently placed the entire project at risk and that a full explanation of the situation would be given at the meeting in Borehamwood.

Driving from the research laboratory in the West of England on this indifferent August morning, I wondered how serious the position really was.

I had first heard the rumour that the project was in trouble through a phone call from my Divisional Manager at home two nights ago. Since then, there had been wild speculation at the plant as to what had happened, but none of us knew anything apart from the disturbing fact that an incredible blunder had been made by the Americans in Washington.

PN49 is a derivative of the well-known and controversial Anglo-French super-sonic transport aircraft the Concorde. Although I have seen some clever press articles in recent months that have come close to guessing the truth, the fact that technological spin-off from Concorde has been used to further the development of PN49 is still classified information.

I think it is the first time that the design techniques used in the manufacture of a civil aircraft have been subsequently employed to assist in the development of a NATO offensive weapon system; the accepted procedure has in the past always been the reverse of this.

Of course, the Americans have poured dollars into PN49, and another well-kept secret was their assistance as silent partners on Concorde, too. Their deliberate reluctance to build an SST of their own is a reflection of their involvement in both the civil and military versions of the supersonic European aircraft.

The Americans are very thorough people and I just could not believe that they had done something at this late stage that would render nearly six years' work useless. If it was true, then the West was in real trouble. NATO had put a lot of faith in PN49 and there was nothing else on the drawing-boards that I knew of that could even hope to take its place for this decade.

Although only responsible for a very small part of the system, the implications of the possible cancellation of the project were serious enough to have caused a knot to form in my stomach that I could still feel now.

The outskirts of London were proving as bewildering to me as usual, and I realised I was in danger of becoming lost. I had allowed myself plenty of time to reach the country house at Borehamwood where the meeting was to be held, but I had not allowed sufficient time to become hopelessly entangled in suburban back-streets.

Accepting the inevitable, I parked the car in a small side road and consulted my map and the instructions that Angela had given me. My wife was born in Elstree and thus had been able to describe exactly the route that I should take. After a few minutes I realised that I was not, in fact, lost — just a little off course. I tried to stop worrying about PN49 in order to concentrate on my driving, but the nagging worry wouldn't leave me alone.

Damn the Americans, I thought — damn

all of them; it was a pity that Europe could not have managed alone.

Besides the expenditure of plain dollars to assist the European main contractors, the considerable technical resources of the United States were vital to the PN49 system. In 1972, two synchronous low-altitude orbital satellites were launched especially for the PN49 project. Each was programmed to pass slowly and periodically over the Soviet Union at a predetermined distance from its sister satellite.

For a duration of two months, very specific and detailed radar records of the terrain had been transmitted to receiving stations in America. When the mission was terminated, a complete set of mapped radar routes leading from strategic European air bases to all major Soviet capitals had been obtained. This was the United States' share of the project, and a part which Europe could not hope to do.

Using simple triangulation techniques, PN49 uses its own terrain-following radar by comparing its route via a computer with the two satellite radar tapes. The weapon system is sophisticated but inexpensive by current standards — it has the unusual virtue of being re-usable. However, without the satellite tapes PN49 isn't worth a bucket of nails — I thought the Americans might perhaps have had trouble in translating the tapes into PN49 format.

Before I knew it, I was outside the impressive wrought-iron gates of the house. PN49 is classified as NATO 'Secret' and even the code name is 'Confidential'. Despite this and recent events, the security regulations were more thorough than I expected.

I opened my pass before handing it through the car window to the uniformed officer at the gate.

He smiled apologetically. 'I'm sorry, Mr Brendon, you'll have to park over there and come back for identification.'

It appeared that security was to be tightened significantly. I parked the company car and walked back to answer all the necessary questions.

As a simple microwave engineer of no great eminence, I was a little surprised to have been invited to such an august gathering of brass. My Divisional Manager was supposed to be here somewhere, but I failed to see him among the crowds on the lawn, recognising only some Ministry men who had attended project meetings at the plant from time to time.

I am rather a shy person and dislike mixing with large numbers of people that I do not know. It was with a sense of relief therefore that I turned in response to a tap on my shoulder to find my old friend Charles Reed grinning at me. Charles works at the Royal Radar Establishment and our association goes back to university days.

He said, 'I didn't think either of us were important enough for this, Richard.'

'Perhaps they want someone to blame it on, whatever it is.'

'No, they can't do that — the Americans are taking the can this time.'

I thought Charles might know more about the meeting than I did.

I said, 'What the hell has happened?'

He shook his head. 'I don't know, but we'll both know pretty soon.' He pointed to the open oak doors of the house, through which people were beginning to filter.

Glad that I had found someone to talk to, we joined some eighty others in a large, dimly lit room in which rows of cinema seats had been installed.

Charles and I found two at the end of an aisle and sat watching the raised platform at the rear of the hall.

Fifteen minutes later, when the foot-shuffling and coughing had died down, a tall gentleman appeared on the small stage, dressed in the uniform of the United States Air Force.

'Gentlemen,' he began at once, radiating the apparent confidence with which Americans are blessed. 'You have been asked to attend this meeting in order to be made formally aware of a serious setback in the NATO PN49 project.'

The click of cigarette lighters echoed around the room as the audience awaited the news.

'Three days ago the first experimental satellite radar tapes were despatched from the United States for the scheduled test flight of the XP1 prototype over northern Europe. They never arrived.'

A subdued burble of conversation amongst the surprised assembly interrupted the speaker.

So the super spies knew about PN49. This was the first time that the project had suffered a security leak, as far as I knew — although alarming, I was not really surprised that something like this had occurred at last.

The man from the American Air Force appeared to be losing his composure a little.

'I have not finished,' he said.

An immediate hush fell over the audience as we waited for the rest of the story.

'With the experimental tapes were the only existing copies of the twelve Soviet attack routes. By an unfortunate error in Washington the entire Soviet route cassette library was included with the experimental tapes and in consequence has also disappeared.'

The knot in my stomach, which minutes ago had felt as though it might soon dissipate, gave a sudden twist.

Beside me I heard Charles say, 'Christ, no,' and everyone started talking at once.

Someone shouted, 'What do you mean, disappeared?' as the Director of the U.K. Weapons Research and Development Establishment joined the now very discomfited American.

The Director was an impressive man and I think held the general respect of everyone in the room. He was Doctor Philip Derwent, and I had met him once when he had visited the lab some years ago.

He peered severely at us all.

Quietly he said, 'Colonel Gill has explained what has happened. It is most regrettable — even tragic. However, I understand that there may still be some hope of recovering the missing tapes. Meanwhile there is a hold on all project work in all countries whilst a complete security investigation is undertaken. I must say that the Department of Defense in Washington is entirely aware of the grave consequences of their foolish error and the C.I.A. are, of course, already heavily involved in the matter.

'Your presence here this afternoon is to make it clear to all of you that the project and NATO have suffered a major blow. To forestall any questions, I will also say that the N.A.S.A. translation team had not made any of the necessary copies before the cassettes left Washington.

'Without wishing to dramatise the obviously serious situation, there is one further thing that I must say. Before this unfortunate occurrence, we had every reason to believe that the Soviet Military Intelligence had a good idea of the strike capability of PN49. You will realise that now they are aware that our principal offensive airborne weapon system for the 1970s has been blinded and made powerless. The position of northern Europe this afternoon is very weak indeed, therefore. I should like you to remember that.'

For the remainder of the afternoon we were briefed about the investigation that was to take place, and instructed on behaviour both inside and outside the confines of the project. An attempt to keep the whole business quiet was obviously a necessity, but I think everyone realised the futility of pretending that it was only us who knew.

During coffee I asked Charles if he thought there was any chance of obtaining new satellite tapes.

'Well, yes there is, at colossal expense. We'd have to orbit another two satellites, but that's not the problem — it's time. We'd never get the information back and translated quickly enough to make PN49 any sort of a threat. It'd take a year before the Americans could even schedule the necessary vehicles for launch.'

I wasn't even sure that PN49 really had a threat potential, anyway. I said, 'It's difficult to believe that a plain aircraft can still be a useful offensive weapon even though it is incredibly fast.'

Charles shook his head. 'Don't forget that at the speeds that PN49 can reach, even if the Soviet radar gets a quick glimpse through the ground clutter they'd never be able to get a lock and track it. And don't forget we get it back — the system is supposed to be for a limited nuclear war, not the full-scale holocaust variety.'

He became suddenly more serious. 'I don't like it at all — I think I'm a little frightened, too.'

I said, 'It seems so incredible that the whole thing is finished.'

'The project you mean?'

'Of course, don't be dramatic,' but my mouth was sour as I said it; you don't make mistakes like this when you're working on projects like PN49.

I knew just how important the disappearance of the cassettes really was. I thought that the eggshell might have the suspicion of a tiny crack. In the last three days the balance of power had shifted just a little, and for mankind, for me, for Angela and the two girls, the future had suddenly become slightly less certain.

2

I telephoned Angela before leaving Borehamwood that evening. The meeting terminated at about five o'clock and I decided to make the long drive back to Bristol at once instead of staying in London overnight.

She sounded pleased when I said I'd be coming home.

'Don't stay up for me,' I said. 'I'll eat on the way down, so I'll be home pretty late.'

'I'll stay up, anyway.'

'Did you manage to get the car serviced?' I asked.

'Yes, and I picked up the new tyre, too — Oh, I nearly forgot, there's a special letter for you.'

'What do you mean, special?'

'Well, it's a thick envelope and it must have come by special delivery while I was out — it didn't come with the ordinary post this morning, and anyway it hasn't got a stamp.'

It would probably be some official notification of the situation on PN49 from the Ministry.

I said, 'Is it on Her Majesty's Service?'

'No.'

'I expect it's from work — I'll read it when I get home; better not open it in case it's about the project. Kiss the kids good night for me — I'll see you later, dear.'

She said, 'Drive carefully, Richard,' and we rang off.

PN49 was going to die hard. There would be other meetings, lots of letters and interminable interviews with the security men from the Ministry; I was not looking forward to the coming months. I wished that Angela and I could get away with the children for a couple of weeks — but that would be impossible now.

I have a special system for driving long distances which allows me to smoke a pipe as often as I like, without having to undertake the dangerous manoeuvre of stoking tobacco when I need at least one hand on the wheel. The system is childishly simple. Before I commence my journey I fill every pipe I own — six in all — and arrange them on the passenger seat in any order that takes my fancy. When the need arises I have only to reach out for a fresh pipe and apply my lighter to the bowl — it is a safe and enjoyable method of reducing the tedium of driving on our congested roads.

My concern about the project, and the possible consequences on an international scale, weighed heavily on me during the drive home. Before I reached the outskirts of Bristol I groped for a pipe that wasn't there and realised that I had smoked all of them. The Triumph 2000 that I had drawn from the company car pool this morning would smell like an incinerator when I returned it tomorrow. I hadn't bothered to stop for dinner — I was anxious to get home and relax.

The Brendon home is not in Bristol itself. Three years ago we bought a small cottage near the village of Chipping Sodbury in order to raise our two young girls outside the pressures of a major city. Both Angela and I like the country, and I suspect our views about bringing up children could be partly an excuse for deciding to live in a quiet rural environment which we enjoy.

Through the curtains, the lounge light shone warmly across the path from the garage. I was very pleased to be home — it had been a hell of a day.

Angela was waiting for me.

'Did you have dinner?'

'No — I couldn't be bothered.'

'Oh, Richard.' She sounded exasperated.

'A sandwich and some coffee will be fine — I'm not very hungry.'

By the time I had changed from my business suit, which is almost a damn uniform in British industry, my wife had prepared a huge pile of sandwiches and was standing in the lounge holding the letter she had mentioned on the phone.

'Go on, open it, Richard,' she said. 'I want to see what's in it.'

I said, 'It's only about the project — and I don't want to know tonight. Come and give me a kiss.'

After I had messed up her hair and behaved as though I'd only been married for a couple of months, I sat down and looked lecherously at my wife.

She laughed at me, throwing the envelope on to my lap.

She said, 'Now, you never know. It might be an inheritance, and then you can retire tomorrow.'

I said, 'Old Aunt Muriel won't leave it to us, and anyway, she's going to live to two hundred.'

But I opened the envelope just in case. It had 'Private and Confidential' written on it in large letters.

Inside were three sheets of thick, good-quality paper. My name was typed at the head of the first one.

I read it slowly, feeling the blood drain from my cheeks as I began to realise the awful truth.

'Richard — what is it — what is it?' Angela had sensed that something was dreadfully wrong. 'Richard?'

I mumbled something to her about it being about my job and took the letter to the bedroom, not trusting myself to look at her.

My stupid mind refused to accept it.

Why me? For God's sake, why had they chosen me?

I took a hold on myself and started at the beginning again. The communication was well written, easy to read, and in no way could I misunderstand the horrifying message lying in front of me on the bed.

It started:

Mr Richard L. Brendon, A.M.I.E.E.,
Project Leader, PN49 Radar System,
Alfriston Lodge,
Chipping Sodbury.

August 26th, 1973.

Dear Mr Brendon,

This letter has been delivered by hand to your home whilst you have been attending the PN49 meeting at Boreham Wood. The meeting will have made it apparent that the project cannot proceed and that the nations of the North Atlantic Treaty Organisation are now at a severe disadvantage when compared with current Warsaw Pact strength.

As you are probably aware, Western

Intelligence reports indicate that the arsenal of Soviet limited nuclear warheads is increasing and that over thirty Soviet divisions (about 320,000 men) are now located in Eastern Europe. Should you be interested in the details, twenty divisions are in East Germany, five are in Czechoslovakia, four in Hungary and one in Poland.

Soviet military doctrine, as put forward by the Commander of the Strategic Missile Forces, states that nuclear weapons of minimal power are to be used to inflict mass casualties only, and that the new policy of the Soviet Armed Forces is to concentrate on hardening of systems with which to fight a European war of a limited nature.

As an intelligent man, Mr Brendon, you will readily appreciate the implications of the loss of PN49 to Europe and to NATO in the present circumstances. It is perhaps unnecessary to point out that conventional ballistic missiles carrying nuclear warheads cannot be used in a limited war without

the attendant risk of full-scale international nuclear conflict.

Thus it is to be expected that you are
rightly concerned at the loss of the
PN49 attack tapes, knowing as you do
that the aircraft is vital to the security
of Britain and other allied countries.

This letter offers you the opportunity
to recover the missing cassettes in order
to preserve the balance of power in
northern Europe.

Whilst it is to be expected that you
are surprised to have been contacted, it
is regretted that no further explanation
can be given here.

The following page contains your full
instructions.

I read the page again, and then again.
My hands were trembling. Angela came
into the room.

She said hesitantly, 'Darling — please
tell me what's wrong.'

I said, 'I can't,' wishing more than
anything in the world that I could talk to
her about it.

'Have you done something terrible?'

'No, it's nothing like that.'

'What can I do, Richard — to help, I mean?'

What the hell could anybody do? Me, quiet old Richard Brendon — they had chosen me for this awful thing. Something that I was going to have to do, and something that was going to have to be done quite alone.

I said, 'Lots of coffee, some of your cigarettes — I'm sick of pipes — and a couple of hours by myself in here.' My wife is an exceptional person. She nodded to me, turned the corners of her mouth up and went for the coffee.

When she came back she gave me a quick kiss and said, 'If there's anything else — I'll be in the lounge.'

I thought I had mustered enough courage for page two now. The instructions were carefully itemised:

R. L. Brendon (PN49) Cassette recovery procedure:

1. August 28th 1973. Proceed to B.E.A. international departure counter at London International Air

Terminal where, by presenting your passport at 1300 hours, your return ticket to Groningen, Holland, can be collected.

2. Sufficient personal effects should be taken with you to allow for a one-night stay in Groningen. It will be necessary to change aircraft at Schiphol, Amsterdam — your ticket contains full details of the flights.

3. Explanations to your superiors at the laboratory and to your wife are left entirely to your discretion; however, it is expected that these will be plausible, as the success of your venture depends on your behaviour being quite normal apart from the necessity for you to embark on this short trip. It is recommended that your destination is not mentioned — indeed, any suggestion of an international trip should be avoided altogether.

4. The security status of PN49 will prevent you from disclosing the contents of this letter to persons outside of the project. However, you

may well believe that it is your immediate duty to contact the Ministry of Defence, who would be able to take steps which would guarantee the recovery of the tapes. Whilst in fact the chance of regaining them by this means is extremely slight, there are other important reasons which will make you wish to avoid contact with any security authority.

Although we would prefer if possible to avoid the necessity of threat, the importance of this transaction requires this letter to present facts which you will find unpalatable and disturbing. Mr Brendon, the safety of your wife and two children is in your hands. In order to preserve their safety you have only to follow the instructions on this page. It should perhaps be mentioned that your telephone is tapped and that your charming cottage is under surveillance as you read this.

Should you decide to ignore these

recommendations it is your family which will suffer and not yourself. We trust that this point has been made sufficiently clear; we have no wish to overemphasise or reiterate this important point.

5. At Groningen, you will be met after flight disembarkation (you will be under close scrutiny throughout the journey) and taken to your destination. There you will be given the opportunity to inspect the cassettes and receive further instructions on subsequent procedure.

Page three outlines the terms of transaction.

My nerveless fingers fumbled awkwardly with the sheets of paper, my mind still unable to grasp the full implications of what my eyes were seeing. The traditional this-can't-be-happening-to-me theme was swirling in my head.

Page three was shorter than the other two.

The PN49 attack tapes are not in the hands of the Eastern Powers; they have been taken for reasons of financial gain by an organised European non-military group. NATO is able to recover them through you, on payment of the sum of one million pounds sterling. Such a sum is considerably below the cost of obtaining new tapes and constitutes only a fraction of the development costs of PN49 to date.

Any attempts by the West to recover the cassettes by force are certain to fail, and at the first indication of a violation of these instructions the entire library will be sold at once to representatives from the Soviet Embassy at the best price.

We look forward to seeing you in two days' time, Mr Brendon. Good luck.

I folded the sheets before replacing them carefully in the envelope. The coffee that Angela had brought me was cold and I was unable to face the thought of a sandwich.

Soaked in perspiration, my damp shirt was cold and clammy on my body and I was unable still to stop the trembling of my hands.

I lit another of Angela's cigarettes, forcing myself to be calm so that I could think.

Two hours later Angela interrupted me. She was trying to smile as she entered the room, but she was tired and desperately worried.

I had come to terms with the situation by now. There was no escape from my responsibilities to my country, to my family and even perhaps to world peace. In two days' time I would leave home to enter a different world of shadow and intrigue — I could hope only that I would conduct myself properly and that I was doing the right thing.

We went to sleep that night with our clothes on and with our arms around each other.

3

The BAC111 landed badly at Schiphol. Although the aircraft was only about half-full, the frightened gasp from the passengers required the hostess to hurry forward to the flight deck in order to suggest that a reassuring statement from the captain should be made over the speakers. If the air pocket along the runway had resulted in a tragic accident to Flight BE193, I wondered what would have happened to PN49. But I was still in one piece and over half-way to my destination in northern Holland.

I had spent all of yesterday at home, trying to convince myself that my duty was to hand over the letter to the Chief of Security at the plant and request full protection for my wife and children. Whilst in some ways such a course of action would have been the easiest solution to the sudden upheaval in my life, I was not surprised to find myself telling Angela that I would be away for a couple of days and that she was not to worry about me.

She had returned the plant car for me in the morning and delivered a note to my Divisional Manager saying that I had personal business of an urgent nature that I had to attend to immediately. I knew there would be no problem at work; in my position I have a good deal of personal freedom, and on numerous occasions have worked at home for weeks on end without questions being asked.

My wife had been more awkward to deal with. Although I have never been able to discuss details of my work with her, she is sufficiently familiar with security regulations to know that something was very wrong in my sudden decision to be away for two days. I think she remained convinced until I left that I was doing the wrong thing, which understandably made it much more difficult for me. To have been able to tell her would have eased the burden enormously, but I could not.

I had an hour to spend at Amsterdam

before catching the F27 that would take me directly to the town of Groningen in Friesland. Before leaving England I had tried in vain to detect my tail, and here, in the busy main air terminal of the Netherlands, I met with equal lack of success. Of course, it was possible that no one had been sent to watch me. I had followed my instructions to the letter, not because I imagined that my every move was being monitored, but because I genuinely believed that it was the best thing to do. It is quite possible that my behaviour had been accurately predicted and that it was considered unnecessary to observe my movements.

To my British eyes, many Dutchmen epitomise my idea of an international spy or agent, and it was almost with a sense of relief that I boarded the Fokker Friendship for the final leg of my journey, leaving the bustle of Schiphol far behind.

There was one stop — at Leeurwarden — two passengers left the plane — and in a matter of minutes we were off again.

Customs and immigration interviews all take place at Schiphol, thus my flight to Groningen was classed as an internal route only. When the aircraft landed, I was able to walk directly from the flight apron to the car park located outside the quaint building that served as a combined waiting-room and restaurant.

At once, I was approached by a stocky man dressed in the uniform of a chauffeur. He had a coarse peasant face.

'Mr Brendon?' — the English was excellent with just a trace of what I supposed was a Dutch accent.

'That's right.'

'The car is waiting, please.'

It was a black Mercedes — an old 180D, the kind used extensively for taxis on the Continent.

'How far is the town?' I asked my driver.

'Groningen is eight kilometres, but we are not going there.'

'Where am I to be taken, then?'

'To Hoogaveen; it is not far — less than one hour from here.'

Somehow or other I had expected to be blindfolded in the accepted manner — surely I was not going to be allowed to witness the exact route which I assumed would lead to the headquarters of this mysterious, but obviously efficient, European organisation. As it would be simple enough for me to lead a subsequent hue and cry to my destination — providing I could remember the route — I could suppose only that the men who had so cleverly stolen the PN49 tapes had no intention of remaining in the area after my visit.

The car had left the main highway now, running over a road of smooth cobbles, lined on each side with mature trees. We had not passed through Groningen town on our way to the country. Traditional Dutch farm-houses, with their beautiful thatched barns, appeared with great regularity along the roadside and I even saw a windmill across the distant fields.

I had not been to Holland before. It was unlike the country of my imagination, being beautiful in its own way because of its flatness, instead of in spite of it. Under different circumstances I would have enjoyed the drive, but the nearness of my journey's end did not allow me to think of anything but what lay before me. I was frightened again and felt cold, despite the warm August afternoon.

My driver had left the second-class country road about a mile back in order to take one which was much narrower, passing through a mixture of sparse forest and heathland. The road was very winding and the surface soon began to deteriorate further. From my watch I knew we were nearly there.

Suddenly the car swung between two massive wrought-iron gates hinged on moss-covered brick columns, and there was a glimpse of two men standing motionless beside a small wooden hut. More trees lined the driveway of the large Dutch house that I could see ahead. I thought that the building would be perhaps two hundred years old and mellow. It appeared a little sinister in its exclusive woodland setting almost devoid of sunlight.

Gravel crunched under the wheels as we pulled up at the foot of the wide stone steps leading to the front door. My driver hurried to help me from the car, insisting that he carry my almost empty suitcase. He rang the door bell, and I waited apprehensively on the step beside him wondering how I was to be received.

The slender gentleman who opened the door appeared to recognise me at once, although I was quite certain that we had never met before.

'Ah, Mr Brendon — I am delighted to see you.'

He proffered a cool, dry hand. 'Please come in.'

There was no suggestion of broken English. If anything, I would have said he was an American.

Rather awkwardly I said, 'I am afraid you have the advantage . . .'

'I am so sorry,' he interrupted. 'My name is Conrad Bessinger — I am your host. Come on and have a drink before dinner.'

I followed him across the spacious carpeted hall to what, in an English country house of comparative size, would be the library or study.

In fact, the room that I entered was

quite small and tastefully furnished in modern décor. Mr Conrad Bessinger went directly to the cocktail cabinet.

'A whisky and water,' I said in answer to his question.

'Now then,' he said when we were seated with our drinks, 'I anticipate a flood of questions.'

I sipped at the whisky, still feeling nervous in the presence of this superficially pleasant man who sat smiling at me from his armchair.

I said, 'Is this your permanent base?'

'Oh, I wouldn't call it a base, Mr Brendon, but yes, this is where we have been working on our little exercise.'

'You mean where you originated the plan to steal the PN49 attack tapes?'

'That is only a very small part of our overall plan, but I quite realise that you cannot be expected to know that. This house is rented from the Dutch Ministry of Agriculture at a very modest rate — our undertaking is perhaps rather more extensive than you might realise at present, and we require a good deal of space which a country house like this can easily provide.'

There was something uncomfortable nagging at my brain, making the sense of well being that was displacing my initial fear a false sensation.

I said, 'You make it sound for all the world as though I am on an official works visit.'

My host leant back in his chair and laughed. His eyes were dark and piercing, set in a sallow countenance. I thought that he would have a quick brain and be a rather cruel man, even though his manner suggested otherwise.

He said, 'But that's exactly what it is.'

'A works visit, you mean?'

'Yes, of course — although I prefer the English word laboratory instead of that obsolete term of the nineteenth-century industrialists; 'works' sounds so old-fashioned, don't you think?'

I took a big gulp of my drink. Mr Bessinger was playing with me and I didn't like it at all.

'When may I see the tapes?' I asked.

'Later — after dinner. You must not be impatient.'

'If I am to check all twelve it will take several hours — especially if your equipment is unsuitable.'

Very special test gear is necessary to check a taped radar record. The easiest way to describe a tape is to compare it to a thirty-five millimetre movie film which has no separate frames. It is a continuous strip of pulsed information, containing a radar picture of the terrain over which the fixed radar beam has been passed.

Whilst familiar with tapes that had been obtained by aircraft flying at very high altitude over the Californian desert, I had never seen a satellite tape and I had certainly no way of telling absolutely that the attack routes were in fact the correct strategic paths to Russian cities. Establishing the routes was not part of my job.

I was, however, relatively confident of my ability to determine whether or not the tapes were authentic, providing the necessary translation electronic equipment was available.

I said, 'Your apparent thoroughness led

me to the conclusion that you would realise the necessity to have comprehensive test gear for me to use. I'm sure you appreciate that I will have to be absolutely certain that these are the correct tapes before I can advise anybody to cough up the million pounds you've asked for.'

Mr Bessinger stood up. 'I can see I will have to put your mind at rest before we go in to dinner.'

He pressed a bell on the small desk beneath the window. Almost at once the door opened and a small Japanese or Chinese moved politely just inside the room waiting for his instructions.

Bessinger smiled at me again. He said, 'Chu will show you our facilities before delivering you to your room. Dinner is at eight-thirty; I will collect you at that time.'

He turned to the silent Oriental. 'Mr Brendon would like a brief glimpse at the guidance test laboratory. He is not to be allowed inside — you understand.'

His statement disturbed me — why a guidance laboratory? Complex test gear I would need, but I hadn't expected full laboratory facilities. Also, his earlier remarks concerning the fact that the tapes were only part of an overall plan, did not fit well into my idea of an organisation interested only in stealing military secrets for financial gain.

The little man was waiting for me to accompany him.

He said, 'You will come with me, please.' The 'please' was lisped badly.

I followed him across the hall, through a doorway, and along a brightly lit corridor. There were no windows.

Numerous closed doors lined each side of the passage. The house was enormous — at least in this direction it was. There was no suggestion of the musty smell that I associate with big old houses — I suspected the whole place must be air-conditioned, although there was no visual evidence of the usual grilles.

Eventually the corridor terminated at a pair of frosted-glass doors. My guide politely swung one open, waiting for me to pass through in front of him.

As I stepped hesitantly forward he said,

'You will watch from inside the door — that is all.'

And there before me was the very last thing that I had wanted or expected to see. I could feel my heart start pounding as, for the third time in four short days, I was confronted with a situation or circumstance that destroyed the orderliness of the secure life I thought I had created for myself.

The room contained one of the best-equipped microwave and electronic test laboratories I had ever seen, equalling those I had been fortunate enough to visit in the major electronic companies of the United States. Right here in northern Holland was enough equipment to develop the most complex system of electronics that could be needed for any purpose whatever.

Mr Chu was anxious for me to leave. He propelled me gently back through the doors.

'What — ' I stuttered foolishly, 'what project is this?'

I received no answer.

Following the figure of the little man

back along the passage, I grappled ineffectually with a jumbled mess of facts. Things were not as I had been led to believe. A million-pound ransom for the tapes was certainly only part of what was going on here. I realised suddenly that I was absolutely terrified of what I had discovered. By no stretch of the imagination had I expected to stumble on an enterprise of this magnitude in this country house, and I wished desperately that I'd never left the sleepy West Country village that was my home.

Blindly, I followed Chu to my room. Before I entered I turned. I said, 'Tell Mr Bessinger I want to see him now, before dinner.'

'Yes, Mr Brendon.' He was behind me, still smiling.

I said, 'To hell with dinner, I want to see the tapes right now. When I've checked them over you can tell me how you want the money delivered, and then I want to catch the first plane out of Groningen.'

Bessinger dismissed the guide, motioning me to accompany him into the room.

He said slowly, 'I regret that you have been a victim of a trap, Mr Brendon. You are not going home — your valuable talents are required here — you have officially defected, Mr Brendon, and your home now is here with us in this building.'

Before I could answer, he swung on his heel and left the room. The door closed in my face and I heard the key turn in the lock. I had become a prisoner, torn from my family that I might never see again, and to all intents and purposes a potential traitor to my country.

With my senses reeling, I lay down on the bed, not able to believe that this had really happened to me.

4

At eight o'clock, whilst still immersed in a whirlpool of despair and self-pity, the door opened and Conrad Bessinger stood framed in the opening. The smile was gone.

I pulled myself together. There was no need to behave as though I was unable to face reality. In the sanctity of my office in the plant it had been easy enough to discuss the accuracy with which the PN49 guidance system could deliver death to thousands of innocent people. I had become involved in a very different part of the same overall armament race, that was all. If I was any sort of a man, I would have to retain my sense of values and adapt to the situation as quickly as possible, not only in order to make sure that I disclosed no secret information to these people, but to maximise my chances of escape.

Bessinger entered the room. He carried

a bottle and two glasses.

He said, 'Mr Brendon — I fully understand your feelings at this time, and I also appreciate that you must regard me with great hostility. However, you are an intelligent man, and I know that if nothing else you will be curious about your predicament and anxious to learn why you have been kidnapped in this way.'

I wished desperately I could appear calm and approach this man on equal terms.

I said, 'I am, but I am not prepared to exchange information.'

'So you would prefer to remain ignorant of our undertaking here.'

'Yes, I would.'

I waited, anticipating the statement which I was sure would come next.

Bessinger passed me a cigarette.

'You know that there is never a choice in these matters, don't you?' he said.

I said, 'Go on.'

'You want me to tell you? It was in the letter.'

'Tell me.'

'Your wife and children.'

So there it was. The universal lever for unwilling defectors. The big stick of Communism that was to be held over me whilst I spilled out the secrets of my country.

I said quietly, 'You bastard.'

Bessinger poured whisky into the glasses, adding some water from the tap before he passed one to me.

He said, 'The destiny of nations has always depended on the sacrifice of individuals — you are only one of many caught by the circumstances that prevail in the world today.'

'I thought this sort of thing was reserved either for government officials with access to large quantities of classified information or for nuclear physicists.'

'In this instance we have need of your experience on PN49.'

'I know little about the actual satellite tapes — you should have collected some experts from the States.'

'We already have the tapes.'

'And what experience do I have that you need?'

The Bessinger smile appeared. 'So you are prepared to discuss it, after all?'

I knew that there was little point in being stubborn. Sooner or later I would have to find out why I had been so neatly trapped, if only to make sure that I did not inadvertantly assist Bessinger and his cause.

Wearily I said, 'Okay, what do you need me for?'

'To complete the development of a terrain-following comparative radar guidance system.'

'Steal the drawings from Bristol.'

'We have you instead — people are easier to obtain.'

'I'm afraid I'm not clever enough to be able to produce a guidance system from my memory.'

Bessinger shook his head. 'I said complete the development — ninety per cent of a working system has already been designed and built by our own staff. You will have eighteen qualified microwave electronic and electro-mechanical design engineers at your disposal in the laboratory here.'

'It would still have been better to have got copies of the drawings.'

The thin man stood up and turned his back to me.

He said, 'The radar system that we require is not identical to that which we understand will be fitted to the PN49 aircraft.'

'How much do you know about PN49?'

'Surprisingly — very little. We do not need to know all about it.'

I said, 'I'm afraid that you will have to be clearer in specifying your requirements, and I suppose I must ask you to be specific about the threat to my family in England, too.'

Bessinger faced me again. He said, 'Although we are anxious to complete our project, experience has shown me that it is unwise to rush matters like this. You arrived only this afternoon and have been subjected to a severe mental shock. Your appearance, Mr Brendon, is that of a beaten man. You cannot be expected to absorb very much more information at the moment.'

I said, 'I am rather weary and also I am very afraid.'

'That is to be expected; it will be some days before you are able to accept the change. I must warn you that escape from the house is not possible. Your present thoughts are naturally centred on your need to return to your own country, and I fully anticipate an abortive attempt to leave the house to be made by you in the immediate future.

When you have been with us for some time, your freedom will be extended to the extensive but fully walled and guarded grounds. Meanwhile I will have to ask you to remain inside.

For the time being you will be allowed only in this room and the technical library. One of my men will be responsible for attending to your requirements and in ensuring that you do not attempt anything foolish.'

By now I was ready to admit that Bessinger held all the aces. I had developed a headache and my stomach was heaving in a series of painful contractions.

Bessinger turned to leave.

He said, 'I will send you up a sedative — perhaps you might be able to eat a light meal as well. Good night, Mr Brendon — I will see you again tomorrow.'

Ten minutes later Chu unlocked the door to find me still sitting on the edge of the bed where Bessinger had left me.

He placed the tray on a chair and left at once.

The smell of the food nauseated me; knowing that it was important for me to try and eat something, I did in fact pick up a fork, but hurriedly replaced it on the tray as another spear of pain shot through my stomach.

If the little Oriental had left the door unlocked — and he hadn't — I would have been physically and mentally unable to make an attempt at escape tonight. I was exhausted, tormented with my thoughts of Angela, frightened beyond reason for little Susan and her sister Anne, and already reconciled to a life of perpetual imprisonment.

With the aid of a glass of water I

swallowed all three of the pills, lay full length on my bed and, without knowing it, slipped mercifully into unconsciousness.

★   ★   ★

My watch had stopped. With no window to my room, I was unable to determine what time it was. At home I am an early riser, waking automatically at about 6 o'clock every morning, irrespective of season or weather.

Awaking from a drugged sleep in an unnatural environment, after what was the most harrowing day I have experienced in all of my thirty-six years of life, I could not trust my feelings that mid-day was perhaps two hours away.

Last night's dinner was still untouched on the chair by the door — I did not think I had been disturbed since Chu left yesterday evening. I carried out a superficial inspection of the room, searching for transmitter bugs or even the hidden lens of a miniature TV camera, but was able to discover nothing. An air-conditioning duct running across the ceiling was not sufficiently large to contain a camera, but it would be simple enough to conceal an audio receiver inside the painted sheet metal. However, I could think of no reason for Bessinger to bug the room for sound, no one had spoken to me, except him, in the short time I had been here and I doubted if I would say anything useful in my sleep.

My stomach felt extremely weak, but thankfully the pain had gone. Two bread rolls and the bowl of fruit on the tray appeared sufficiently appetising for breakfast and improved my view of things somewhat.

On the washstand stood my suitcase — or rather Angela's — it had A.B. embossed on the lid. She would be expecting me home today.

I had a shower in the adjacent bathroom, cleaned my teeth, and shaved with my cordless electric razor.

When I re-entered the bedroom Conrad Bessinger was waiting for me.

Sufficiently refreshed to take the initiative, I said, 'Good morning — may I ask how you knew I was awake?'

'Although I control the movements in this house, Mr Brendon, I regret that I have no magic which allows me to know when people leave their beds. I came simply to wake you up; it is eleven o'clock.'

He was wearing a white laboratory coat over a brightly coloured yellow shirt, making his already pale face even less attractive in the artificial light of my room.

I said, 'I should like to continue with our conversation. I want to know exactly where I stand.'

'I am afraid I have a meeting this afternoon with some visitors. However, if you wish, we can go to my room where we can discuss the project for the remainder of the morning.'

'And about my wife and children?'

'Mr Brendon, your imagination is quite capable of telling you why your family is still dependent on your work. You appear to want me to embark on a subject that we will both find uncomfortable although regretfully essential.'

'Would you hurt them?'

'Yes.'

'Kill them?'

'If necessary, but . . . '

I interrupted, 'But you won't if I finish the design of your bloody radar?'

He motioned for me to leave, joining me in the corridor outside.

'Please come to my room.'

Bessinger's room turned out to be an office adjacent to the small study that I had been in yesterday.

He sat behind his desk after pulling up a large swivel chair for me to sit on.

I said, 'I cannot for the life of me believe that I have or know anything unique about radar systems. Yes, I have been responsible for PN49, but it is the satellite tapes that are the heart of the whole unit. I am quite sure — in fact, I know — that the Soviet Union have sufficient technical expertise to develop a system without requiring help from me.'

The damn smile appeared again. One day I would take great pleasure in wiping it from his face.

'Ah, Mr Brendon, you are an impulsive

man — you are jumping to conclusions again.'

'What conclusions?'

'The thirty-seven people in this charming Dutch house — a number which includes both you and me — represent the political and military interests not of the Soviet Union but the Great People's Republic of Communist China.'

'What?'

'China, Mr Brendon — Red China, in Western parlance.'

I was unable to conceal my astonishment. There was a long silence whilst I unravelled the tangle of preconceived ideas that had been accumulating in my head. These men were not instruments of Russia, not controlled by masters in the Soviet Union — I had fallen into the hands of the Chinese, the growing power in the East that was the enemy of both the Western Allies and of the U.S.S.R.

Bessinger said, 'I thought you would be surprised, but I expected that you might have guessed.'

'No — I automatically assumed this was a Soviet operation.'

'I think, Mr Brendon, that you were correct in your assumption of a moment ago — the Russians would have no need of your talent.'

'Are your staff Chinese?' I asked him.

'Only three — we have very mixed nationalities here, but we are all dedicated to the cause of the People's Republic. The Netherlands are remarkably tolerant with regard to immigration of foreign nationals, but a concentrated group of Asians in a remote country house would attract too much attention and be suspicious, to say the least.'

It was incredible — I found it hard to believe that Peking had stretched out its inscrutable arm as far as northern Holland and from there could affect the entire defence strategy of western Europe.

I said, 'And Red China wants its own PN49 with the Soviet attack routes already made?'

Conrad Bessinger shook his head. 'Not exactly — it is rather more complicated than that. I should like one of my colleagues to explain the political situation to you briefly and then outline the concept of our own project which the People's Republic have established here.'

The faithful Chu — quite obviously one of Bessinger's three Chinese — responded to the bell push.

Bessinger spoke to him in Chinese — at least, I supposed that it was.

'Do you speak Chinese?' I asked him.

'Poorly, I am afraid.'

I wondered where a man like Bessinger would learn Chinese, but had no opportunity to ask before the political expert arrived. He was a large chunky man — I guessed of Indonesian extraction and therefore very acceptable in Holland.

Bessinger explained, 'Major Salajar is aware of your recent arrival and of your function. He will endeavour to describe our aims — I trust you will not be bored.'

The Major sat down stiffly, inspecting me closely as he began to speak in a dull monotone. His English was almost perfect, and readily understandable.

I was subjected to twenty minutes of ridiculous propaganda about the might and the glory of the wonderful People's

Republic of China — the sort of thing that is universally mocked in the United States and in England. If I had not been so desperately worried about my position and about Angela, it would have been difficult to avoid laughing.

Throughout this initial introduction, Bessinger stared solidly at the blotter on his desk top, his hands flat and motionless in front of him. It was impossible to believe that he could agree with such exaggerated rubbish.

After half an hour he interrupted the Major.

He said in English, 'Excuse me, Major, but I have arranged for some coffee at this time — perhaps you could resume afterwards.'

Chu brought in the tray and there was silence as we drank.

Before the Major could begin, Bessinger said something to him that I couldn't understand.

Then Bessinger turned to me. 'The Major will now explain current Chinese strategy in Europe and define our purpose. I think this will be what you will really want to know.'

I accepted a cigarette, pushed the thoughts of my home to one side, and made ready to concentrate on what was to come.

5

The second part of Major Salajar's speech was delivered in a less efficient manner. It was immediately less boring and more believable.

He began hesitantly, 'Both the Soviet Union and the members of NATO are regarded by the People's Republic of China as major powers conspiring individually to overthrow the Chinese Government. Further, both powers are developing means of neutralising each other's increasing armoury of nuclear weapons. In particular, my Government believes that Russia would have no compunction in levying total war against China in order to prevent us from developing further military forces and weapons. This is a situation which will not be tolerated.'

I knew that part of what he was saying was correct. In some sectors of the West it was genuinely hoped that a Chinese-Soviet war would erupt, if only to reduce the threat to North America and Europe.

He continued, 'Our acceptance as a member nation to the U.N. allowed us for the first time to meet the challenge on equal political terms. Before this, steps had already been taken to guarantee the defence of my country, despite the fact that we are only recent members of what is called the nuclear club. Unfortunately, we are very short of I.C.B.M. capability, although small numbers of mid-range ballistic missiles are already operational on our borders.

'Two years ago, the growing military strength of Japan began to be of concern in Peking, and it was realised that we could not hope to keep pace with all the nations of the world in the armament race. As we could not afford to fall behind, either, long-term strategic plans were formulated, which would guarantee the survival of the Chinese people, opposed as they are on all sides by hostile enemies wishing to destroy the mightiest nation that the world has ever known.'

I said, 'PN49 — or your version of it — is part of your strategic plan?'

He ignored my remark, pausing only to light a cigarette.

'My government, deciding therefore that drastic action must be taken, undertook a study into methods of combating this oppression by the utilisation of our limited resources. One clear and unassailable solution presented itself at once and, in this house — close now to final completion — is the culmination of years of strategic and scientific study. A system that will guarantee the survival of my country for ever.'

I sensed that I was close to discovering the reason for my abduction.

The Major's voice rose.

'Early next year, the world will know that the People's Republic is the major force and that it is impossible to threaten our ancient race — when the twoheaded snake strikes, China will lead for evermore.'

He was almost shouting and his English had become worse — I despised him for his tiny military mind.

Bessinger was saying something to me. I said, 'What?'

'Mr Brendon, the success of our venture and the survival of China can be materially assisted by your presence here.'

Angrily I said, 'For Christ's sake, what is it you want of me?'

Bessinger smiled slightly. 'Simply to modify our guidance system so that our carrier vehicle can fly in both directions along the routes from the satellite tapes.'

'You mean make the radar able to control an aircraft from Russia back to its home base?'

'Exactly.'

'What the hell for?'

'In January 1974 twenty-four drone aircraft, powered with modern pulse jets, will leave central Europe — each fitted with nuclear warheads of medium strength.

'Twelve will follow the attack paths established by the American satellites to Russian cities. The other twelve will follow the routes in the reverse direction to the European air bases from which your PN49 was to be flown. Drones will be launched at time intervals which will guarantee that all explosive devices detonate simultaneously.

'Thus, Mr Brendon, our simple inexpensive drones will be used to pursuade the Soviet Union that they are under attack by the Western forces, at the same time as NATO concludes that Russia has launched a nuclear attack on all strategic European air bases.'

'No,' I shouted. 'My God, no — you can't — you can't!'

These men were planning world war — deliberately setting out to cause nuclear war between Russia, Europe and her ally the United States.

I was standing up shouting at the two men sitting in the room. 'You're mad — insane — completely bloody mad!'

My fists were clenched — I wanted to kill both of them, but something was telling me to take a hold on myself; and it wasn't fear of what would happen to me or to my loved ones. As far as I knew, half the world was innocent of the plan to incinerate its people by atomic war. Their future — perhaps the future of Western civilisation — depended on whether or not I could prevent this awful thing from happening.

Bessinger said, 'Sit down — there is nothing you can do.'

'You honestly expect me to help you?'

'You will.'

'No!'

'Your family.'

'Four of us in exchange for half the world — not a bad bargain.' I felt sick as I said it, seeing Angela, Susan and Anne dead before my eyes.

'You are not indispensable, Brendon,' Major Salajar said dispassionately. 'You have co-workers, but they are not essential either. We can complete the work here without the help of your damned technicians; it will simply take longer, that is all.'

I sat down limply. Bessinger passed his cigarettes. 'You will do it.'

I didn't answer.

Bessinger said, 'Perhaps you will understand why we are here in northern Holland now. From here we can program our drones to lock on to the attack routes which are being plotted from the tapes at this very moment. We believe that our pilotless aircraft will not have far to travel before they pick up the defined routes that the satellites have so cleverly recorded.'

I said, 'You can't realise what you're doing — you can't.'

Major Salajar said, 'I have already explained — we are guaranteeing the continued survival of the Chinese Republic. We will be left as the sole major power in the world whilst Europe, the U.S.S.R. and the U.S.A. lie in total radioactive ruin. It is a bold plan — the Chinese do not play games.'

I was about to deliver a stream of ill thought out invective to Major Salajar, which might have relieved some of the incredible pressure that was rising inside me, when there was a quiet knock on the door.

An elderly bespectacled gentleman — I guessed he was another Indonesian — entered in response to Bessinger's 'Come in.'

He carried a large roll of paper.

He addressed Major Salajar. 'You will please to excuse this intrusion, but you asked for the inspection of each plot as they are translated from the American cassettes.'

'Yes, yes, yes.' The Major was angry to have been interrupted. The man with the map coloured slightly.

Bessinger stood up and held out his hand for the roll.

He said, 'You were quite correct, Professor Djambi — perhaps you would like to show all of us.'

The Professor said, 'I have spent nearly all of the time on checking the translation equipment and developing the new pulse receiver — she is only two routes complete.'

Salajar corrected him rudely. 'I have completed only two routes. Speak properly.'

'Yes — I am sorry — two only.'

Bessinger unrolled the paper on his desk. It was a map of the world — one of great detail and of superior quality.

The intolerable mixture of sick despair, rage and fright reduced inside me a little as I became interested in what was before me.

Two thin red lines wound their way

across the top quarter of the coloured map. For the first time I was about to see two of the routes that the satellites had plotted by radar. Routes established partly by geographic experts, partly by espionage agents advising NATO of long-range Russian radar installations which must be avoided, and by careful study of actual photographs taken by the old U.2 spy planes of the nineteen-sixties.

With great curiosity, I studied the gentle curves and twists of the lines, noting carefully the location of the ends.

On a Van der Grinten projection, some of the lines would be compelled to leave the right-hand edge of the sheet before reappearing in order to reach the far eastern section of Russia, but both of these lines terminated before the need for this. With a start I realised that I was automatically following the lines from west to east. My years with PN49 had conditioned me to attack routes only in that direction. Now I would quickly have to adjust my old ideas and learn that these red lines were not unidirectional. Chinese drone aircraft were going to travel to each end of these routes, carrying screaming death to Russians and Europeans alike. It was difficult for me to be objective in my study of the map with such thoughts in mind.

One of the lines began — or ended, depending on your point of view — at Le Creusot, just south of Dijon in France. I knew that Le Creusot was a major NATO air base where the Americans had stationed Phantom fighter bombers — it was a logical start point for PN49. The other end of the line terminated precisely on Leningrad. This particular route passed well south of Hoogaveen, almost missing Holland altogether, but as inter-continental distances are quite large, and as pulse jet drones are relatively quick, it was probably no real disadvantage.

I had to push between Bessinger and Major Salajar in order to follow the second line backwards from the Russian city of Kirov to the south of England. And then I could see.

The air and naval base of Portsmouth was scheduled to receive one of the drones. I could imagine the enormous, expanding, searing ball of raw energy melting the concrete of the dockyards and fusing steel and stone together. The screams of blinded, still living people echoed in my ears as I stood silently in this quiet Dutch country house, coldly looking at these insidious winding red streaks of death.

Bessinger spoke. 'And how long before we have the remaining ten, Professor Djambi?'

'Now that the pulse receiver she is good, I hope for not more than one day for each.'

Salajar said, 'Good — please proceed as quickly as you can.'

When the Professor had left, Bessinger addressed me with no trace of the smile. 'I think you understand now,' he said.

I nodded.

He said, 'It is pointless to sacrifice your family and ultimately yourself as well. As the Major has said — there are other engineers from your plant and we are competent to finish the job ourselves if necessary.'

Bitterly I said, 'My wife and children will die anyway when the war is started by your warheads.'

'Ah, Mr Brendon, that is the other end of the bargain. We can threaten them on the one hand but save them on the other.'

It was no good; the recurring mention of my wife and my two precious, innocent girls in the same context as this ultimate evil was having its effect. There was a welling surge inside me as I tried with all my might for control.

The fragrance of Angela's hair, the softness of her body; the laughs of my children on a warm, sleepy Sunday morning in the garden. The bark of a distant farm dog, our home, our family — my family. All gone forever whilst I laboured as a captive to bring about destruction and death to a major part of the world. Not even killing myself would arrest this terrible machine — escape was the only answer. I must obtain help, help that would wipe these men from the surface of the earth, leaving not even a bloody smear to regenerate such evil again on this earth.

I turned on the two men, two alien men, puppets of a country governed by monsters.

My control was slipping more quickly now.

I shouted meaningless abuse, conscious that intelligence and reason had finally deserted me and that my behaviour was that of a man at the end of his mental tether.

A red film flicked transiently over my eyes, and my body was burning up as I raved.

Then I turned and ran.

Blindly, I rushed across the hallway and down the steps from the front door, my legs pushing me forward with a force born of intense hatred combined with paralysing fear.

The long, straight driveway stretched before me. On the rough gravel surface I ran, with my breath beginning to rasp dry in my gaping throat.

As in a dream I saw the black iron gates swing slowly together to block the passage of my headlong flight. But I could fly and if I couldn't fly I could climb with the energy of a man possessed with the strength of madness.

Dimly I saw the wooden hut beside the

gates. The sentries made no attempt to stop me. I was going to escape, no one could prevent it.

And then, in a prelude to my final climb to freedom, I threw my body at the frame of twisted iron.

The high voltage threw me backwards like a toy. I hit the soft grass beside the driveway, to sink and drift into the absorbent solitude of total darkness.

6

The muscle of my arm was painful where I was lying on it. It still hurt after I had laboriously rolled over on to my back. I was in bed.

Vainly attempting to focus my eyes while struggling simultaneously to remember where I was, I picked out the outline of a figure of a man standing over me. Dragging myself into a state of full consciousness was a slow process, taking so long that I could detect the awakening of my senses one after another.

I was back in my room and the man was Bessinger.

He said, 'He is awake now — that will be all, Doctor.'

Another man, one that must have been behind me on the other side of the bed, walked quickly to the door, leaving me alone with Conrad Bessinger — the man who was to lead half the world to utter ruin. He was holding a hypodermic syringe in his right hand.

I touched my arm, noting the beads of blood gathered on my finger.

He said, 'You have rested for a long time and it is necessary for me to ask you some questions. Are you fully awake now?'

My mind was becoming clear and alert — perhaps too clear. I tried to sit up, discovering that as yet the condition of my body in no way matched the feeling in my head.

I said, 'What was the injection for?'

'You have had two — one to calm you after your irrational attempt to escape, and another — five minutes ago — to wake you.'

'Just to wake me?'

'Mr Brendon, you have still only been here for a very short while; during your brief stay you have learned of our plan to help preserve the security of the People's Republic of China and have attempted to reject the idea of your participation in our activities. In order to make quite sure that our progress will not be interrupted, it is important for us to learn something of you. In particular, I have to satisfy myself that you left no information in England that could in any way disrupt our important work. I have asked our resident doctor to administer a drug that will help me obtain the answers I need.'

I knew what that meant. I said, 'How long have I been asleep?'

'You were brought here after receiving the shock from the main gates at mid-day. It is now the morning of August 30th. And now I must begin.'

I toyed with the idea of refusing to answer, but only for a moment. The exceptional clarity of my brain induced by the drug might help Bessinger get the answers, but it also materially assisted my powers of reason — or did it?'

It had been made quite clear that development of the Chinese guidance system could continue without me if necessary. I was required only to acceler-ate their program in order to meet some sort of deadline. A refusal to co-operate would immediately put Angela in danger and reduce my own chance of survival, too. It was vital for me to escape from here to warn the Western powers and there would be more chance if I pretended to submit to their requests.

Bessinger said, 'What did you do with the letter that was delivered to your house?'

I had to make a swift decision — God, it was difficult. I chose the truth.

I said, 'I arranged to have it delivered to a colleague if I didn't return within one week from the time I left England.'

'I see — that was rather stupid of you after our warnings.'

'I had no idea then whether or not it was a wise decision.'

'You realise now that the safety of your family depends on you telling me exactly how to recover the letter before it is delivered?'

I said, 'Yes, I realise.'

'Does your wife have it?'

'Yes, but she probably doesn't know it yet.'

'Please explain.'

'Angela shops once a week — she went on the day I had to attend the PN49 meeting because I didn't need the car. I arranged for her to collect a new tyre from the local garage. She told me they had fitted an ordinary one instead of the radial type I had ordered. The following morning I telephoned the garage to say my wife would return the wheel in a week's time so that they could replace the tyre. When the tyre is removed from the boot of the car, my wife will see the letter I have left for her in the well.'

Bessinger smiled. He said, 'I see, and what is she to do with the letter?'

'I wrote a brief explanation to her explaining what had happened and said she was to deliver your letter to Charles Reed at the Royal Radar Establishment. Reed is a friend of mine.'

'Is that all?'

'I also told her that her life and the children's might be in danger.'

'But you are confident she will not have discovered it yet — don't forget she was expecting you home yesterday.'

I said, 'I don't know.'

Bessinger's gaunt features and his smile made him look evil somehow. Now I knew what he was part of, it was impossible to believe in the pleasant smile that was almost constantly flickering at the corners of his mouth.

He said, 'Your wife received a telegram from you late yesterday afternoon saying you had been delayed. It was signed, 'Love, Richard' — I trust that is a normal method of signing off in the Brendon family?'

I didn't answer.

'You will appreciate that it was important for us to have this little chat before your wife becomes alarmed. Also we expected you to have arranged a small insurance policy. I must say, Mr Brendon, that you chose a somewhat unimaginative method of guarding yourself against a situation like this.'

'I was in no frame of mind to plan anything ingenious.'

'No, I suppose not. We will arrange at once to recover the letter from your car. At the same time we will be pleased to deliver a letter from you to your wife and children. You will say that you are safe but that your future existence depends on them behaving in a normal manner in so far as that will be possible under the circumstances. I will return to collect the message from you in one hour — pen and paper are beside your bed. Do not attempt to be clever or devious in what you say or you will have to write it again. Breakfast will be brought to you when I have left.'

He tossed the disposable plastic hypodermic into the wastepaper basket in the corner of the room, pointed to an unopened packet of cigarettes that had been provided by the management and left me to write my letter.

The temptation to attempt a coded message was enormous. Every married couple have their own special language for use in privacy, and without having to be too obscure I think it would have been possible to tell Angela where I was. Nothing could be gained from such a move, however, so I avoided the mention of anything that Bessinger might regard as suspicious. I ate breakfast as I scribbled.

Shortly before I finished writing, an extremely loud noise made the table vibrate under my hands. It was a continuous low-frequency howl — rather like a large single-cylinder motor-cycle engine being revved to death. After a few moments I realised that it must be one of the pulse jet motors under test somewhere in the grounds outside. I thought it was noisy enough to attract attention from traffic passing the house, even though the road was some distance away. It distracted me from my letter.

Bessinger reappeared before I had finished writing. He sat on the bed, waiting.

When I had finished, I passed it to him for approval.

'I will read it later,' he said. 'Come, I will show you one of our delivery drones — doubtless you have already concluded that the noise is from one of the pulse jets.'

Ten minutes later I was standing behind the protective safety glass of a fully instrumented test house, located about a quarter of a mile from the house.

The drone was much smaller than I had expected, being about twenty-five feet long and a slender three feet in diameter. Like the old German V1 missiles used in the last world war, the engine was mounted on a pod, but the nacelle had two pulse jets in it and was slung beneath the main fuselage instead of above it.

Although I was wearing ear-plugs like the six other people in the control-room, the noise was shattering. I had endured it long enough when Bessinger motioned for us to leave.

When conversation proved possible again, I asked him why pulse jets had been chosen instead of other forms of propulsion.

'I am afraid I am not able to answer your question in an authoritative manner — our vehicles have all been supplied from the People's Republic — however, I believe they are of Russian origin — rather ironical, don't you think?'

'They were supplied to China in the days when your country was being aided by the Soviet Union?'

'Yes, I think so. China received large numbers of Russian 'Guideline' tactical missiles and several of these pulse jet drones. We have sold the missiles to Albania — our own are greatly superior now — but the drones have been reserved for this particular job.'

From their appearance, I thought the altitude/speed characteristics of the drones might approximate quite well to PN49. If there was a wide discrepancy in speed or manoeuvrability, it would be very difficult to use the satellite tapes.

With a shock I realised that I had begun to think of what techniques it would be necessary to adopt in the radar receiver to compensate for different carrying vehicles. I would have to be careful not to become too interested in the engineering problems. Escape was my project — I could permit no other interests to distort my sense of values. And yet I would have to exhibit some degree of interest in order to safeguard Angela until the time came for me to make my break for freedom.

I said, 'Do you have all twenty-four drones here?'

Bessinger nodded. 'All are already completely operational and housed in underground sites here in the grounds. Each one is tested every month. Only the comparative unit of the terrain-following radar has to be fitted before they are ready for use.'

'What about warheads?'

'We have eighteen, I think it is — the remainder are expected in September — at least we will not have to test them.'

The sun was warm on my back as I walked back to the house talking to Bessinger about the technical problems that I could foresee. It seemed incredible that, in such a very short time, I had been wrenched from my job, my family and my country, to be plunged into a totally foreign environment which I was already partway to accepting as an inevitable, if unpleasant, facet of our times.

It was lunch time before all my questions about the control servos and flight responses of the drones had been answered in Bessinger's room.

Sandwiches were brought by Chu at exactly one o'clock. Bessinger said, 'This is the last occasion that you will eat with me here. This afternoon you will be introduced to the other members of the staff and you will join all of us in the dining-room for your meals from now on. The food is excellent — you will have no complaints, I am sure.'

There was something to come before the promised round of introductions. I had been with Bessinger long enough since my arrival to be able to detect emotion through the mask of his pale face.

When the sandwiches were finished and we were smoking our cigarettes, he began talking again.

'Mr Brendon, there are certain regulations which I am compelled to follow in the administration of this organisation. You are not a patriot of the People's Republic and have been forced — yes, forced, I think, is the word — to assist in a venture that you cannot be expected to approve of. In cases like yours it is usual to have periodic reminders of the reason for your cooperation. Every week, it will be necessary for you to report to Major Salajar in the library to view a film that has been compiled by our agents in

England. The film will be the same on each occasion as long as you continue to work well. If you are suspected of deliberately dragging your feet, you will be warned by me once and once only. Should the warning fail to improve your performance, a new film will be taken which, as before, you will be required to view weekly. This process is a continuing one; however, I am told that experience of this technique applied to American and British scientists and engineers shows that there is never need for more than one additional film to be taken.'

I was both curious and frightened at Bessinger's description of the so-called technique.

I said, 'You don't approve of the method?'

'I did not say that — I said merely that it is necessary for me to enforce the regulation which applies to all defectors.'

'I'm not a defector.'

'Do not argue. Come with me, please.'

Salajar was waiting for us. A sixteen-millimetre projector sat on the library table, a beam of white light shining on a screen at the far end of the room.

He said, 'The film runs for seven minutes and the quality is poor.'

With great apprehension I waited whilst Bessinger closed the door and switched off the lights.

There was no title, only a list of four names — mine, Angela's, Susan's and Anne's. I had an inkling of what was to come.

The first scene showed my two daughters leaving the school bus at the corner of our road in Chipping Sodbury. Taken from a parked car on the other side of the quiet street, it was not easy to pick out close detail, but I knew who the little girls were without the need for a telephoto shot.

As soon as they began to cross the road I saw the black car fifty feet behind them. It was parked, but the body was gradually tilting to one side as I watched. I knew why. It would be fitted with automatic transmission, and the driver had one foot on the brake and the other hard down on the accelerator. The transmission was literally winding up with the torque, causing the whole car to tilt on its suspension. When Anne and Susan were half-way across the street, the driver of the black car must have removed his foot from the brake.

Although the film was silent, I could hear screeching tyres as the car shot towards the two small figures in the road. The girls must have heard, too. Susan grabbed at her sister, pulling her desperately forward. At the last minute, when the car dominated the screen and I was on my feet screaming, the driver swerved, missing my children by perhaps a foot or maybe two.

I sat down sweating.

The scene with Angela was less harrowing. I was treated to the sight of a high-powered rifle being loaded and subsequently levelled at the figure of my wife as she undressed one night in our bedroom at home. The film was taken through the telescopic sight, providing a close view of Angela's bedroom routine. Mercifully, the poor quality of the film revealed nothing — but a touch of a trigger and Angela would have been dead.

I watched in silence, my hands gripping the unyielding wooden arms of my chair.

When the film had finished, I thought that no one could frighten me any more about anything. In a few days I had been exposed to potential catastrophe at every imaginable level; there wasn't much else I could be confronted with.

Nothing was more certain than the fact that I had to escape, but until I did there was going to be no need for anyone to make another film. I thought that the second film would probably finish with a cast of two instead of three and that was not possible to contemplate.

I said to Bessinger, 'I'll work.'

And I did.

7

Conrad Bessinger was an easy man to work for. He had a brilliant brain and was not lacking in humour, although it took some weeks for me to appreciate his cynical wit. In the U.K. or in the States he would have been a very successful engineer, ranking with the best that I have ever met. His staff of qualified personnel in the house were equally intelligent, but lacking in the experience that my colleagues in England had been fortunate enough to obtain on other projects.

As he had said, the nationalities of his team were very varied. Unlike Bessinger, they were universally indoctrinated with Chinese Communism to the point of fanaticism, and I quickly learned to avoid any reference to political differences in my conversations with them.

Despite the unusual circumstances surrounding my employment, I was treated, at least on a technical level, with the greatest deference, being regarded as a specialist in the field of weapon-guidance radar. It was difficult for me not to form the usual attachments with the engineers who worked for me; they were a congenial enough group of men, dedicated to their project and by no means preoccupied with the end result of their labours.

Not all of the staff were concerned directly with the radar. Apart from those in service functions, such as the doctor I had seen shortly after my arrival, numerous people were responsible for the many aspects of the twenty-four separate launch complexes. There was a department to deal exclusively with the security of the house and one to issue formal reports to the Dutch Government. The official front for our enterprise was so unlikely that I was surprised that an enquiry had not been instituted by the authorities long ago. For over three years the house had been rented from the Ministry of Agriculture for the purpose of establishing a secret missile base to blow Europe and the Soviet Union into little pieces. And for three years a totally artificial organisation under the name of the Society for World Political Unity had spewed out document after document from this house, aimed with great singularity of purpose at convincing the Dutch Government of the authenticity of our work to unite the nations of the world. All of the information for the reports, which were written in Dutch, was supplied from Peking — modified slightly if necessary, and printed locally in Hoogaveen. The quality of the documents was superlative and the contents very believable. Masterfully executed with a minimum of work at our end, the front had performed flawlessly for the entire time that the house had been occupied.

The periodic burst of noise from the pulse jets occurred only when the wind was in a favourable direction. Furthermore, the grounds surrounding the house proved a good deal larger than I had first supposed. In all, over twenty acres belonged directly to the residence, whilst, to the south, was an extensive area of low-lying swamp interspersed with trees.

The trees, in fact, were something of a nuisance, requiring the initial flight paths of the drones to be close to vertical.

About half-way between the house and the south fence of the property, the underground launch silos showed their presence only by gentle mounds of earth at the twenty-four exits. Each silo was connected to the automatic launch director system situated in the basement of the house. The director handled all of the pre-launch check-out routine for each drone and would automatically arm each warhead before firing the vehicles in the required time sequence. Drones would fly by simple radio control to their selected route, before the full terrain-following radar would take over the guidance by comparing its ground picture with the satellite tape carried on board.

Since seeing the two routes on the map that Professor Djambi had shown Bessinger, I had not been given the opportunity to view the remaining ten that had been subsequently plotted. Not that the information was of vital importance to me. Knowing that London was to receive a nuclear warhead of medium strength early in 1974 would be of limited usefulness even if I did escape.

January 22nd was the date for the launch. Bessinger told me that certain moves were already afoot to increase tension between the United States and the Soviet Union. Using their new position in the United Nations, Chinese delegates were beginning to re-create a rift between the two countries. Major Salajar indicated that a tension level similar to that experienced in the Cuban crisis was aimed at.

The longer I worked at Hoogaveen, the more I became totally convinced of the success of the project. The free world depended for its future existence on Richard Brendon, and Richard Brendon was not up to the job.

I had my own office, a laboratory assistant and everything that I could possibly require to complete a thoroughly sound and well engineered guidance system. There was no chance of sabotaging the electronics or the microwave package. My subordinates were too astute for me to even consider such a move.

For over two months I had spent eight hours a day, five days a week in the laboratory, poring over wiring diagrams, circuits and prototype units. The similarity with PN49 was uncanny even though I was quite sure the development had proceeded separately as Bessinger had said. My job therefore was not difficult and there were times when I felt satisfied with a particularly neat solution to a technical problem. It was only back in the sterile loneliness of my room that the horror of what I had done would steal coldly into my stomach, causing me to reach for the pills that Bessinger had provided.

By now I had freedom of the house and of the grounds. There was a small penalty to pay for this very real contribution to my health and sanity. Around my left ankle I wore a small steel clip. Inside the clip was a small fixed-frequency radio transmitter, allowing the shift man in the security department to pinpoint my whereabouts at any time.

Usually the clip was worn as a bracelet,

but in my job, where I was working with extremely high voltages on laboratory test rigs, the risk of a fatal shock through the metal was much too high. So the clip was modified to fit my ankle. And then it was riveted on. Salajar and Bessinger jokingly referred to it as a twentieth-century ball and chain — it was apt enough, I suppose.

My weekly visits to the library to see the film soon became afternoons to which I eagerly looked forward. Because I knew exactly what I was to see, it was easy to ignore the message of the action and enjoy the opportunity to see my dear family. The bedroom scene of Angela too often appeared to me in sexual fantasies at night, but apart from this rather minor distortion, the film was a material help to me in providing a weekly reminder of what I had left behind. It was also a comfort to realise that Chinese psychologists had made something of a mistake in believing that the horror content would have a lasting effect.

Early in my captivity, I had made up my mind to postpone my escape until I could be sure — absolutely and utterly sure — that my bid for freedom would succeed. I believed that there would be an optimum time for my attempt. For the first few months I could be reasonably expected to be restless, frightened and unstable. I was sure I would be carefully watched throughout this period. Then, as the launch date drew nearer, they would expect the tension in Richard Brendon to increase and surveillance would once again become more intense.

Thus somewhere between the beginning and the end of November would seem to be the most suitable time. However, as the days and the weeks passed by, I became conscious of the need to delay my escape. How much of this was reluctance to embark on a task of such enormous importance, and how much was genuine belief that the time was not yet ripe, was difficult to tell. I am not a brave man and the burden of responsibility of this particular job was such that no man, no matter how brave, should be asked to carry it.

Rather foolishly, as time passed, I tried

to convince myself that it was Angela and the girls whom I must save as being more important than the nameless millions who depended on me as well. I suppose this was an irrational attempt to scale down my problem to comprehendable proportions and natural enough, but I feared that the process might continue until it was my own skin that became of prime consideration. Before that happened — if it was going to — I would have to be gone. Gone from this civilised quiet life of technical endeavour that would end — if I were to let it — in an event that I had ceased to contemplate many weeks ago.

As it happened, my mind was made up for me. I could postpone the matter no longer. I had been guilty of encasing myself in a protective cocoon of false security. The pleasant manners of my colleagues were seen suddenly, not to be false, but to be those of total foreigners — alien in thought, purpose and intent.

It started on November the twentieth when Major Salajar came to my office in the morning to say Bessinger wanted to see me.

I said, 'Tell him that I can't until the modulator output test is finished.'

Salajar and I did not like each other. He was a non-technical man and resented the apparent freedom that I had.

He said, 'You will go now.'

'I've told you — no.'

Picking up my telephone, he dialled 61 — Bessinger's office. To annoy me, he spoke in Chinese.

After a few moments, with an exaggerated bow, he handed the instrument to me.

I said, 'Bessinger — the oil-cooled modulator is outputting into a dummy load right now — I want to watch the temperature rise myself; we've done this twice before without recording it and there isn't time to do it again.'

His voice was impersonal. 'How long will you be?'

'A couple of hours.'

'Please come to my office as soon as you have the results.'

I said, 'All right,' replacing the receiver and looking pointedly at the waiting Major.

For the first time I had really got under

99

his skin. He spat rudely into my wastepaper basket and said something that I was sure was very rude before turning to leave.

I said, 'The people of the Republic have extremely bad manners today,' but he didn't stop.

For the next two hours I busied myself with the test, not turning off the equipment until I had plotted the curve of the temperature rise on a graph.

I told the mechanical section head to open up the unit when it had cooled sufficiently, and to leave it open until I returned. Then, satisfied with my morning's work, I went to see what Bessinger could want.

He was behind his desk waiting for me. He had what I called his hangman's expression on his face. His thin lips were compressed and his complexion was paler than usual.

I sat down, waiting.

'Mr Brendon,' he began slowly, 'you will remember that you and I, or rather you and the People's Republic of China, have a bargain.'

I had long ago given up trying to persuade the staff here to say China instead of using the cumbersome full title that they had given their country. Bessinger, I could see, was in no mood for a reminder that P.R.C. would be an adequate abbreviation.

'What exactly do you mean?'

'You no doubt recall the conversation where the safety of your family in England was discussed?'

With sinking heart, I nodded.

'And you remember that no further film will be shown to you providing your performance is satisfactory?'

'I've done nothing,' I said wildly, 'I swear to you I haven't done anything at all — you cannot have reason to believe otherwise.'

Bessinger stood up. He said, 'I must issue you with a formal warning. This will be the only time. After this a new film will be shown to you.'

I was on my feet now, sick to my stomach with fear.

'What have I done?' I asked. 'For God's sake tell me what it is.'

'I think you know. Both Major Salajar and I have discussed it at some length before deciding to issue this warning. Induced fear may temporarily affect your work output, but in the long run we believe that the project will benefit from this brief chat here this morning.'

Despair was clutching at me.

Weakly I said, 'I swear I do not know where I have failed — you must tell me now or I cannot rectify my shortcomings. Bessinger, tell me — please tell me.'

'You may return to the laboratory now — there you will be able to think — but do not think too long — your effectiveness is more important to your family now than ever before.'

I opened my mouth, but I knew the subject was closed. They had perversely chosen not to tell me.

With faltering steps I went to my room. My mind in its present state would be of no use in my work and I could not now afford the smallest, most insignificant mistake.

8

It was several days before I reached the conclusion that I had in fact committed no sin, except perhaps to have become too complacent about my performance and position. In order to remind me of the importance of my work, they had chosen to issue a warning. Whether or not the next fatal step would be taken I had no way of knowing, but I dare not take the chance. In some ways I genuinely believed that they would not choose to murder one of my children or my wife. With only three months to go, to subject me to such a shock would be stupid, especially as I was quite sure that they were in reality satisfied with my work.

Nevertheless, the warning frightened me enough to make me begin actively formulating my plan for escape. Since my arrival, I had taken every opportunity to observe and remember the smallest scrap of information that could later be used to help me. Now it was time to weld these together into a foolproof scheme which would cover every eventuality and, as far as was possible, guarantee the success of my vital mission.

Apart from the escape itself, there was the decision as to what to do thereafter. My escape could not be expected to remain undetected for very long, and I expected Bessinger to mobilise every staff member in a desperate bid to find me before I contacted the authorities. For the sake of retribution or plain revenge, he might even pass the command to kill my wife and children immediately. I imagined that he could telephone instructions to England, and there was no way I could prevent him from doing that once I had left the house.

Grappling with these thoughts for many nights, I reached eventually what seemed to be the best solution to my problem. There was no easy answer, everything was a compromise depending on how accurately I could predict Bessinger's behaviour and how efficiently I handled myself.

I had considered what I believed to be every possible method of leaving the house and grounds. From the inner recesses of my mind, I drew on my memories of every escape book I had ever read.

During the last world war, so many ingenious escape ideas had been employed by large numbers of prisoners of war that it seemed incredible that none of the methods would apply to my predicament. But, none of them would, and I was left to originate my own plan to scale the wall.

For some weeks I had considered the possibility of riding out on one of the cars that were used to collect supplies from Hoogaveen, but there were too many weak spots, even in the most superior plan that I thought of. It would have to be the high brick wall with its single strand of barbed wire that ran along the top.

The major complication arose from the certain knowledge that my escape would have to be undertaken at night. A curfew was imposed requiring me to be inside the house before sunset, and in my room or in the dining-hall or laboratory for the remainder of the evening. Thus, not only would I have to negotiate the wall, but first find a way to silently leave the building. All of the windows were barred — not, of course, just to keep me in — but to prevent curious outsiders, who might manage to penetrate the outer defences, from breaking into the house. The front door was locked at all times, both from the inside and the outside, and I was the sole resident without a key.

During the day I was accompanied frequently by Chu who, while having a certain dog-like charm in the way he followed me about, was, as a conversationalist, a total failure.

I would have to leave at night, I would have to steal a key, and I would have to climb the damn wall. To complicate matters, before I could do anything, I would have to get rid of the tell-tale clip from my ankle. Unless I did that, I could be traced so easily that I would have no chance whatever. Wrecking it, so that it could no longer transmit, would be fine — once I was well away from the house and grounds. However, if things went wrong too early, the missing bleep from the clip would be a certain indication that I was up to something. It would be better by far to leave the transmitter in functional condition somewhere that would not raise suspicion.

And so, I continued to think, exploring avenues of escape in my mind that ended too often in a brick wall — frequently literally so.

November passed with the days chilling noticeably now. Hoogaveen was significantly cooler at this time of year than the West Country of England, and there were times when the air-conditioning in the laboratory was working hard to maintain the required temperature.

On December the third I undertook a small experiment. The grounds of the country house abounded with a small variety of rabbits which, earlier in the autumn, had served to amuse me in my lunch breaks and in the evenings. Using a snare made from thin steel strip and a length of electrical wire, I successfully caught a fine male specimen some hundred yards from the house. The width of the metal strip prevented the usual unpleasant death from strangulation, the little chap being quite unharmed but very frightened when I collected him in the evening.

Although he was kicking furiously, carrying him beneath my jacket without being seen was not too difficult and I soon arrived at the perimeter wall. Tying the wire from his new collar to a handy bush, I connected it to a much longer length taken from my pocket. Then, with the aid of a stone tied to the end, I swung the wire upwards towards the top of the wall. When the manoeuvre was complete, my rabbit was connected positively to the innocent strand of barbed wire on the top of the wall.

I left him there that night, revisiting the site of my experiment during my coffee break on the following morning. There was still frost on the ground in the shadow of the wall and the grotesque twisting of the limbs on the small body could be seen in contrast with the white ground as I approached. Round the neck, where the collar touched the brown fur, a large burn mark told its story.

As I expected, when the gates were closed at night the barbed wire became very much more dangerous. Knowing the gates were open now, I pulled down my connecting wire, noting that it had fused to the barbed strand at the contact point when electrification had been switched on last night.

I felt unreasonably sorry about the rabbit. It had been sacrificed to save humanity, but it was still a waste. The pathetic little body lying on the cold ground was the opening scene of a ruthless act that was yet to come, although on that December morning I had no way of knowing what lay before me.

On December the fifth my laboratory assistant was kind enough to leave his jacket in my office when, together with the other engineers, he went to fetch our morning coffee. It took exactly fifteen seconds to obtain an impression of both sides of his front door key in a carefully prepared layer of hard plasticine.

By December the seventh the fingers of

both my hands were blistered and sore, whilst my nail file was completely smooth on one side. I had used emery paper, scissors and a nail file to produce my key. It was made from six separate laminations of thin sheet steel, which were bonded together with the special epoxy resin we used in the laboratory. Starting with thin sheet, it had been possible to rough out the blanks with scissors, thus avoiding the necessity to remove large quantities of steel with the file.

That night I tried out my masterpiece whilst standing casually by the door, a newspaper in my hand. The subterfuge was somewhat transparent. I couldn't read Dutch, and everyone knew I could not. Nevertheless, I was undisturbed throughout the experiment which, rather to my surprise, proved entirely successful, the key feeling as though it was worn to fit the lock from continual use.

In my bedroom, hidden in the mattress of the bed, was a contraption of which I was rather proud. Made principally from string and pieces of wood gathered from my walks outside, I regarded it as a small piece of insurance which could possibly make all the difference or, alternatively, be a complete waste of time and effort. It worked in conjunction with my wastepaper bin and my shower.

Before leaving my room for the last time, my ankle clip would be attached to the business end of this ingenious device. I would turn on my shower, leaving the water trickling into the metal wastepaper bin suspended below the nozzle on a stout length of rubber tubing. As the weight of water increased, the bin would progressively trigger a series of cords and weights as it descended gradually to the floor. Each cord was in turn connected to my clip, with the result that over a period of an hour the transmitter would swing from one corner of the room to the toilet, from there to the centre of the room and from there to the washstand. It was my belief that displacement of the clip could be detected by the security watch at this close range, and I hoped therefore that this movement would be regarded as normal, should I inadvertantly cause myself to come under special attention at any time during the evening of my escape.

My remaining escape kit was somewhat simpler. Twelve feet of heavy electrical cable had been stolen from the laboratory, to which was secured what could be described as a grappling hook manufactured from the wire coat-hangers from my wardrobe. Also stolen from the lab was another essential part of my escape equipment — a roll of thin synthetic rubber sheet roughly one-eighth of an inch thick, four feet wide and about six feet long. It was used to provide an insulating surface to the bench tops, and spare rolls were readily available in the small store near my office.

To complete the kit, I had collected six bars of chocolate, a short thick-bladed knife — the kind used to cut linoleum — and a strong pair of side-cutters. I still had my passport, but I had no Dutch money, only seventeen English pounds which would be of limited value until I reached a town where they could be exchanged.

With this pitiful collection of articles, I

— Richard Lloyd Brendon — was hoping to save half the world from oblivion. No prisoner from the concentration camps in Germany during World War Two had carried such responsibility, and yet escapes were made from escape-proof compounds with less equipment than I had. The motivation of those men was the simple need to be free, free to fight again. In my case, the motivation to escape was of such enormous proportions that on several occasions I was conscious of totally rejecting the concept of nuclear war in the northern hemisphere. I wanted desperately not to know that it could happen, and, above all, wished either that I was dead or that I could approach Bessinger with a plea. For Bessinger had made it clear that there was a possibility that my family could be removed from England to join me in Canton before the war was started. I had only to volunteer my services to the People's Republic for the remainder of my life to save my family from certain death.

I had avoided discussing the matter with him in detail, but twice — after my warning — I had thought how easy it would be to have given in and defected properly to the Eastern Power who held me captive.

On December the fifteenth, after dinner, I retired to my room, laid down on my bed, and told myself that the time was near. I had left my attempt too late for comfort, but I was not conscious of increased surveillance — perhaps because I had made a deliberate effort to exhibit very regular daily habits. Chu had relaxed his vigil, knowing that I could be found at the same place at the same time on every day. Also, in my frequent chats with Bessinger I had attempted to convey the impression of being slowly convinced of the inevitability of world domination by the Chinese. On Mondays, when I attended the film in the library, I took the opportunity of explaining to the good Major how I wished I could come to terms with myself and agree to work for the People's Republic in the future, saving my family into the bargain.

Major Salajar was not of the same mental calibre as Conrad Bessinger and I believed that my somewhat transparent ploy was believed with only slight reservation.

Periodically, I suffered from headaches; they have plagued me all my life. Not the paralytic migraine type, but sufficiently serious to prevent me from leaving my room for up to a day at a time. All of the staff here were aware of this debility and accordingly, when I mentioned that one of my damn headaches was bothering me earlier in the afternoon, I received genuine sympathy from the engineers in the laboratory. Before leaving the dinner table I made a point of reminding everyone that I was not feeling well, refusing the offer of a cigarette in order to reinforce my statement. I still smoked my pipe that I had brought with me to Holland, but had taken to consuming anything up to a packet of cigarettes a day as well. Although my nerves appeared not to have benefited by this increase in smoke consumption, I was conscious that my health had deteriorated slightly as a result.

Now, lying on my bed, I inhaled deeply, telling myself that tomorrow would be a better day, and knowing that if I postponed my escape until then it would be too easy to wait for yet another day — and then another, until the weak, frightened thing that I would become went crawling to its masters whining to be saved.

It was now or never.

I rolled off my bed and stood up, looking at myself in the mirror, feeling more alone than I had ever done before. My hair was a little greyer at the sides, I fancied, and the wrinkles in my forehead that Angela liked seemed deeper now. This night — December the fifteenth, this year of our Lord nineteen hundred and seventy-three — was the night that Richard Brendon had to make his contribution to the rescue of humanity. I hoped the Lord was watching.

As I moved around the room, methodically erecting the motion simulator for my clip, I tried hard to concentrate on Angela, using the memory of my wife as an anchor for my thoughts.

The side-cutters from the laboratory were Soligen steel — made in West Germany and the finest I had ever seen — the Chinese always bought the best equipment. I used both hands on the plastic-covered grips, exerting enormous pressure on the first rivet that held my ankle clip together. The rivet head snapped off, rocketing across the room to bounce off the far wall. I moved the cutters to the second rivet, then to the third and finally to the last one. There was a moment of panic when I thought the steel jaws would not reach the final link that secured the transmitter to my leg, but suddenly it was free, and I was free from its evil signal.

When the clip was tied to the long cord hanging from my light in the centre of the room, I pulled it towards the shower, fastening it in its initial position. Next, I withdrew my escape kit from the hiding place behind the washstand and laid it on the bed. Stowing the various pieces of equipment in the pockets of my warmest clothes was the work of a moment — I had rehearsed this part of my plan for many hours in the preceding days.

Five minutes later I was ready. There was nothing more to be done now. My watch said it was five minutes to ten — the time that I had chosen as optimum from over twenty evenings of careful observation. At nine-fifty-five there were fewer people in transit across the hall than at any other time of the day. Those who could understand Dutch would be waiting for the news in the television-room, whilst some of the others would be in the library for the last cup of coffee or tea of the day. The remaining staff members would either be working or in their rooms reading.

Opening my door, I listened for the sound of conversation or footsteps. Then, satisfied that all was well, I went quickly to the shower and turned on the faucet.

Catching sight of myself again the mirror caused me to pause — just for a moment.

I stared at the reflection, wondering that I had finally summoned the strength for what I was about to do.

Then I whispered, 'I'm coming now, Angela — I'm coming home,' turned abruptly and left the room, closing the door quietly behind me.

9

By the time I reached the south wall I was shivering. The chill of the night and my screaming nerves combined to rack my body with a series of long shudders.

A slight breeze was rustling the leaves along the base of the dark solid buttress in front of me, making it difficult to hear any noises that could be coming from the house.

The key had worked perfectly. My fears that on the real night it would jam or delaminate whilst still in the lock had proved to be nothing but fears. And no one had seen me leave the house. All I had to do now was climb the cold, lonely wall to be free.

Unwinding the coils of heavy wire from my body was a welcome relief. I laid the cable on the ground, checked the attachment of my grappling-hook and prepared myself for action. Then with one long, slow swing the steel hook was over the top row of bricks — mercifully just missing the lethal strand of electrified wire. My cable was heavily insulated, but I would still have balked at the idea of having to unhitch it should I have been unlucky enough to have snagged the barbed wire strand.

I had taken the trouble to tie a series of loops in the cable for my feet, not trusting my ability to climb a raw cord only half an inch in diameter. It was still difficult though, and my knuckles scraped painfully against the rough bricks as the cable swung from side to side under the action of my upward movement one foot at a time.

Still rolled up, the rubber sheet was gripped firmly by the end in my clenched teeth. My jaw began to ache painfully from the strain before my head drew level with the top of the boundary wall.

There was not time to look, but I could not restrain myself. In the dark it was difficult to determine how dense the forest was, but I knew that the trees were in large clumps with swamp land in between them. It was a good choice

— better than the north wall with the gate, and better than the east and west walls which bordered on open farm land.

Steadying myself, I shook free the roll of rubber. With one hand on the top of the wall, I used the other to cast the sheet upwards. My first attempt was a failure, the folds cascading down over my head. Learning from experience and urged on by the knowledge that my foot was being slowly cut through by the loop of wire that was supporting my weight, I tried again. This time the sheet unfurled properly, forming a safe, electrically insulated cover over the barbed wire.

Gingerly I used the remaining loops to climb further upwards, leaning my weight forwards on to the rubber, knowing my throat was not more than a fraction of an inch from voltage sufficient to kill me in an instant.

Further I climbed, until at last my feet could stand on the top row of bricks. Very slowly, I lifted one leg to step over the rubber-covered wire, only to find that the move was impossible without having something to stabilise myself with whilst balancing on such a narrow shelf.

I should have laid down and crawled underneath it — there was just enough room and the danger negligible. But the manoeuvre was physically complicated, especially when having only a narrow strip of crumbling brick on which to balance. So I gingerly sat on the wire, unavoidably loading it downwards by the weight of my body. The high voltage was now at a position on my person that didn't bear thinking about — I hoped fervently that one of the barbs would not puncture the sheet to conduct the killing energy into my genitals.

I had managed to find a toe hold and was in the process of lifting over my other leg when there was a loud ping and the rubber sheet collapsed in a crumpled heap between my feet.

There was just enough time to collect myself for the long jump before I toppled. As I fell forward one of the broken ends of the barbed wire brushed across my clothes.

I landed well — it was not far to the ground and the soil was soft, absorbing most of the shock.

Cursing my incredible stupidity for applying so much load to the wire, I began to run the hundred or so yards to the dim shape of the trees in front of me.

Half-way there, through the sound of my laboured breathing, I heard the bell in the house. I had never heard it before, but it needed no imagination to know that the loss of continuity in the electrification circuit had been detected automatically. The bell was an alarm. My escape had been discovered already — almost before I had cleared the wall. Worse, the broken strand, the rubber sheet and the climbing cable would all show without question which way I had gone. I had planned to take the rubber and the cable with me, in order to avoid leaving any pointers behind. Now I had fouled up everything, and I was sick with fear, trembling and weak at the knees.

Forcing myself to think was inconsistent with the instinctive urge to run until I dropped from exhaustion. When I reached the trees, almost sobbing with exasperation, I stopped, realising that my reasoning ability was all that was going to save the situation — if indeed it was not too late already. My moving clip might still buy a little time. Perhaps they would search the grounds first, thinking someone had tried to break in. In the dark it would take a long time to find the break in the wire unless they had an electronic refinement that would lead them straight to it. Or would they search for me at once? Bessinger was at least as shrewd as I was — if not more capable — and he was not terrified half out of his wits.

It was a matter of priorities. I couldn't take the chance with Angela and the girls. Although Bessinger was certainly not Chinese, he had enough of their inherently cruel characteristics to order the murder of my family without a second thought. I had to warn my wife of the danger as soon as I could. To do that I would have to evade capture and make my way to somewhere that had a telephone. Then I would approach the Dutch police with my story so that steps could be taken to destroy the drones. The chances of rounding up the members of the Society for World Political Unity were probably remote now they knew I was at large, but that was of secondary importance to me.

But I was not safe yet. Objectively I knew that I should be prepared to sacrifice my loved ones if necessary. It was more important to inform the authorities of this nest of vipers in Hoogaveen than to save my family, and I knew I should concentrate on that. Nevertheless, the brief pause to get a message to my home could not really hinder my overall goal — there were perhaps only hours to warn Angela — whereas the destruction of the missile sites was not of such immediate urgency.

I was brought to my senses — ripped out of these academic thoughts — by the lights; lights that fortunately were concentrating on the grounds of the house. From the roof of the old mansion, beams of white light were reaching out into the darkness, sweeping past the walls and occasionally flickering over the top.

Hidden in the trees, I could just see the searchlights moving first one way and then the other, in a series of long, slow arcs. If I had been inside the confines of the wall, I would have been picked out in an instant.

Realising that it was only a matter of time before the search would expand outwards, I took a final look at the grim scene behind me before walking hesitantly into the cold stillness of the trees.

My exertions over the past ten minutes or so had warmed me a good deal, but I still shivered occasionally. There would be a frost tonight; I could feel the crispness of the ground under my feet where the trees were thinner. It was very dark and very quiet.

Hoogaveen lay to the north — in the direction of the house. It was my intention to travel south far enough to be well clear of trouble before striking off either to the east or west in an attempt to find a road. My knowledge of the geography of Holland was poor, being restricted to what I had learned from a small map the evening before I had left Chipping Sodbury. Nevertheless, I knew Groningen was a town of significance where it would be simple to find some official organisation who would be able to protect me whilst my surprising story could be told. But I couldn't wait until I reached Groningen before somehow getting a message to Angela — I couldn't even wait until I reached Hoogaveen.

I had adopted a fast walk as the best compromise pace at which to travel. It was rapid enough to make me feel as though I was progressing at a satisfactory rate, yet involved little danger from collision with trees and branches that I could see only faintly in the dark.

Within seven or eight minutes I emerged from the gloom to find a drainage ditch stretching away on either side of me. Scrambling down the steep grass-covered side was easy, but the water and the mud at the bottom was much deeper than I had expected. By the time I reached the opposite bank I was wet, muddy and exhausted.

Worse, I was conscious of a new noise that was drifting across the silent Dutch landscape. With a sinking heart I realised it was the sound of starting cars.

Bessinger had reacted with commendable speed. My escape had been discovered and the Chinese were mobilising to scour the surrounding roads for me.

I was under no illusion about my future were I to be caught. They knew now that I was not to be trusted and I was no longer useful to them.

Most of my work was at a stage where it could be taken over and completed well before the launch date, now only a few weeks away. If they found me I was a dead man, and the world would never know the vital secret I carried.

My legs were beginning to ache with the strain of pulling one foot after another from the waterlogged ground. I thought that it would have been easier to travel if the mud were frozen. But it wasn't and it was no good wishing it was.

The flatness of the Friesland country-side allowed me to see quite some distance, and it was not long before the headlights of moving cars about a mile and a half away to my right told me where the nearest road was to be found.

Knowing I would have to choose either

between the highway or continuing across country hoping to find a farmhouse, I stopped for a moment to think.

It was then that I heard the splash. Something or someone was crossing the ditch I had negotiated three hundred yards back.

A coldness crept into my stomach. I dropped to the damp ground, fumbling for my knife. I could not afford the delay — I had to contact Angela before Bessinger's assassins were sent to kill her.

Then my peripheral vision picked up the faint figure in the distance. There was no doubt they were after me in earnest across country and by road, knowing that unless I was captured their project was finished and so were they. Their masters in Peking would not tolerate a mistake of this magnitude. They had to find me, and quickly.

I assumed that they would have fanned out from the point where I had climbed the wall. There would be more than one of them.

But they hadn't reckoned on the change in the quiet microwave engineer from England that they had kidnapped. In fact, the feeling that was creeping over me as the man approached across the field was one that I thought was not in me. Slowly, hatred was overtaking my senses and I was conscious of a building urge to suppress the years of training that had taught me to use my head, tongue and pen to make my way through life. In this situation something else was needed.

He was less than fifty yards away now. From time to time he switched on a powerful flashlight, but it was directed on the ground, presumably in an attempt to pick up my footprints in the mud. It must have been easy for him to have followed me once he had found my track leading from the trees.

I was hugging the coldness of the grass, wondering at the stream of fear that was being smoothly withdrawn from my body as if by a giant hand. The hairs on the nape of my neck were erect now — something that hadn't happened to me before, despite moments of blind fear that I had experienced previously. A Richard Brendon was in the making that I didn't know — a cold, cruel, fearless and hating person. I tensed as he approached across the wet grass.

The fool didn't see me until I sprang to my feet and launched myself violently forward.

A long animal cry was torn from my lips and I seemed to tower above my enemy, thrusting aside his ineffectual attempts at defence.

And then the wicked curve of my knife was in his belly, pulling viciously upwards, his warm blood spurting over the fingers of the man that had driven him to eternity.

The body sank to its knees and toppled on to my shoes. He was dead before he hit the ground.

I kicked the head away, noting without pity the wide-open, sightless eyes staring to the sky. Inside me the hate was still cold and hard.

There was no more shivering, no weakness at my knees and no remorse. I had killed a man, but, at that moment, it meant no more to me than if I had crushed an ant beneath my foot.

I wiped the knife on the grass, picked up the flash-light and disengaged the silenced automatic from the fingers of the dead man. His hand was warm and moist.

The change had come at last. To save countless millions from the horrors of nuclear war called for a man who understood that life was not always sacred. Suddenly I had become aware of the real rules — it wasn't a cold war, it was a simple matter of plain survival, and inside me now the necessary instincts had finally developed.

Alert and armed, fully conscious of what I was doing, I moved on, leaving the man I had killed behind me in the silent loneliness of the cold field.

10

I headed directly for the road. Already the frequency of passing headlights was reducing as the night crept on, not more than one vehicle every ten minutes moving across my limited horizon. Despite this low traffic density, I was sure that I would find my way to a telephone more quickly by attempting to thumb a lift than by stumbling about the Dutch countryside hoping to come upon a farmhouse.

More of Bessinger's men would be in the general area, I was sure. They would not have sent a single man to follow my trail from the wall. I knew very well that I could not afford to walk blindly towards the road across such open country.

By lying low on completely flat ground I had been able to surprise the man I had killed before he had even suspected that he was close to his prey. In this game it was the moving man who was vulnerable.

Warily I moved slowly towards the gentle mound of earth that skirted another irrigation channel. Then, crouching slightly, hoping that the slight cover would reduce my chance of being detected by a distant watcher, I followed the low bank to the west in the general direction of the highway.

Periodically I stopped to listen, wishing that I dare use my new flashlight to reassure myself that I was indeed alone in this bare, cold landscape.

The warmth induced by my earlier exertions was beginning to dissipate now and nervous perspiration started to form icy rivers inside my shirt. I was not frightened of another encounter with Bessinger's men, but I was becoming increasingly anxious about my lack of speed in finding a telephone. Whether my family were to live or die could easily depend on how quickly I reached the road. I was certainly not going to be excessively cautious in making progress for this reason.

I had covered about half of the distance when the headlights of a car drew to a halt at a position directly in line with the ditch that I was following. Simultaneously, to my right, I saw a quick flash of light from the centre of the dark pool that was the field I had recently crossed.

Sinking from my crouch to the grass that bordered the bank, I stopped at once. Without a doubt they were using radio communication to carry out the search for me. Either the car had stopped at the request of the man with the light who had undoubtedly signalled his position, or the car was a control point and had asked for a location check. If I was right, the radio silence of the man I had killed would be highly suspicious and a more intensive search of the field might be carried out in the next few minutes.

Unfortunately the night was not really dark enough for my purpose. Scudding clouds were varying conditions so that I could not rely on a particularly dim period during which I could move forward. I could not risk exposing my figure to the Chinese who were hunting me.

Although not an expert on firearms, I had enough of a working interest in them to know that the one I carried was a Walther P.38. It was reassuring to feel it in my hand and I decided that I would continue with my original plan, being ready to kill again if the situation demanded it.

A moment before I moved on, the beam of the flashlight from the man in the field stabbed out towards me, temporarily blinding my vision. Almost immediately it swung away in a slow arc, probing the shallow depressions and tussocks that were in its range.

I was sure that the starting point of the search pattern had been coincidence. If it wasn't, the beam would have lingered, illuminating me and making me a sitting duck. On the other hand, if the man who was manipulating the light was clever — and I hadn't met anyone at the house who wasn't — he could easily have moved the beam away as soon as he saw me, pretending I had been unobserved.

My stay at the phoney headquarters of the Society for World Political Unity had shown me the foolishness of embarking on such mental gymnastics. Trying to out-think someone of almost exactly the same intelligence level can be an impossible exercise. The double, treble or even quadruple bluff calls for great concentration and plenty of time, and I had neither at the moment.

I eased myself over the bank into the cold water of the adjacent ditch, realising at last that I had been lying beside a foolproof route to the highway which would allow me to remain hidden for the entire distance that I had to travel.

The noise of my legs moving through the slush would of course advertise my progress to anyone with keen ears, but the man with the light was too far away to hear, and noise was less dangerous than exposure of my person.

After a quarter of a mile the near-freezing water was having its effect. The depth varied from about six inches to two and a half feet, causing me to stumble dangerously at times, completely soaking the lower half of my body. I became conscious of a numbness that was slowly creeping upwards from my feet.

Twice I imagined that I saw someone

lean over the top of the channel ahead of me, and twice I had been at the point of switching on my light with the Walther ready to fire. But, on each occasion, the last half-second of restraint had been enough to show me that the figure I had imagined was formed from sparse groups of rushes that grew along the way.

Eventually, almost paralysed with cold, I scrambled up the south bank of the ditch to discover that I was but two hundred yards from the roadside. The car had gone.

Yet another watercourse lay between me and the grass verge that I expected to line the highway. One final minor obstacle to overcome before I was back in touch with a small part of civilisation and one step nearer to total freedom.

For two or three minutes beside the ditch from which I had recently emerged, I lay wondering where the enemy might be. Had the car picked up my follower or had he been joined by others? Where were they now? Would they expect me to head for the road?

Flipping the safety catch off the

automatic, I stood up, gazed quickly around me and began to walk to the dark tarmac strip.

No sooner had I taken my first step than I knew I had made the fatal mistake of underestimating my opponents.

On each side of my ditch, between me and the road, I saw them stand up. As if playing with me, their flashlights remained off whilst we stared at each other, waiting.

I wondered if they knew I had killed one of their comrades and was now armed with the automatic.

Then suddenly the rays leapt forth, blinding white, changing the darkness to an unbearable spangled burst of light.

Knowing that I had only seconds to live, yet strangely unafraid, I reacted in the only possible way.

In one cat-like leap, the Walther bucking in my hand as the silenced muzzle spat flame towards the lights, I was back in the protective darkness of the ditch.

My eyes were useless, the irises closed against the fierceness of the flashlights.

Fighting the instinct to peer along the channel for a glimpse of the enemy, I screwed my eyes shut, willing the apertures to expand so that I could see.

When I opened my eyes again I could see a little better, but certainly not as well as before. It would be many minutes before good night vision returned.

I could not stay here — not below ground level, with the Chinese free to range on either side of the ditch, waiting to kill me like a rat cornered in a hole.

Then I heard them. Two splashes and a muttered curse told me that they were in front of me in the channel, waiting. There were no lights.

Pressing my side into a shallow depression on the south wall, I strained my eyes into the dark shadows. Further splashes drifted towards me. They were approaching, taking care not to use their lights now that they knew I was able to kill at a distance.

Gambling on the thin hope that they would not expect me to have a flashlight as well, I waited for them to draw closer.

The same calmness was with me again.

This was a job that I must do and do it well — if I didn't, I was a dead man and the agony of nuclear war would overtake mankind.

They were brave men. Knowing that a bullet could come from anywhere along the bank to snuff out their lives could not be a pleasant thought, yet still they came on.

For me to move now would be extremely dangerous. The gentle swish of the water in this uncannily still environment would give my position away in an instant. I had no alternative but to wait until I could be sure of my targets.

Despite my apparent calmness, I was acutely aware of my heart beating more quickly than usual and I felt almost unnaturally clear headed.

Minutes passed. Three times they stopped, making me wonder if one of them had climbed out of the ditch to walk along the top. By the time my eyes told me that I was not imagining the movement in the shadows, my enemy was in range.

I counted to twenty before switching on

the powerful light, flicking it rapidly from one bank to the other. This time the advantage was mine. Both men were blinded, caught in the searing white beam. Realising too late that he was lost, one of them panicked and began to climb desperately up the slippery mud of the bank. I levelled the Walther, steadying my hand whilst I squeezed. A semi-automatic is an ideal weapon for close work and three times my finger touched the smooth curved metal of the trigger. My first bullet took the climbing man in his thigh, preventing him from moving further. The second entered his trunk, just above the waist, and the third smashed sickeningly into his heaving chest.

Before he was dead his comrade had recovered enough to open fire, the period of time that I had held my light stationary on the dead man allowing him to switch to the attack.

Dull orange flame licked out of the shadows, bullets thudding horribly into the mud all around me.

My flashlight was off now, neither of us

wishing to take the risk of giving away our position to the other.

I had no real idea where he was. He was certainly not stupid enough to have remained where I had seen him last and, each time he fired, the flame from the muzzle of his gun appeared from a different position.

Still leaning against the muddy wall, gripping the Walther, I stretched out my gun hand towards the centre of the ditch. Then, systematically, I began shooting, trying to cover as much of the cross-section of the dark waterway as possible.

At once my enemy retaliated, the shots seeming to come from low on the water as though he was lying down.

After five shots I quickly withdrew my outstretched hand, put the warm automatic in my pocket and started to climb the side of the ditch. I gained the top unscathed. Then, covered in mud, I put my head down and ran for my life towards the road, weaving on the frosty turf, expecting to feel the bite of a bullet at every step.

Negotiating the channel bordering the

road was easy; I had become very experienced at this in the last few hours.

Looking back, I could see no sign of the man behind. I thought he might perhaps have given up the chase.

The incredible change in Richard Brendon — sometime engineer and now an undisputed killer — still did not seem to be of dramatic importance to me. I wondered if I was in a state of shock or whether there were hidden resources in me that I had never known of before. Whatever it was, I had come to feel just a little smug about my performance so far — and then the old sickening fear for Angela crept back to envelop me.

Tired now, with the same old desperate feeling inside once more, I began to walk northwards to Groningen and Hoogaveen.

I elected to stay close to the security of the ditch that ran parallel with the road. If the man I had left behind had radioed for assistance, there would be great danger in signalling any car that might conveniently appear within the next few minutes.

During the next quarter of an hour I

retired twice to the darkness of the roadside whilst cars sped by, wondering if, in the interest of speed, I should take the chance or not.

When I was on the point of deciding to attempt to stop the next one, another pair of headlights appeared in the distance. This time there was a difference. The two spots of light rode higher from the road surface than the others I had seen — they would be those of a heavy truck.

In plenty of time I stepped out into the centre of the road with my muddy flashlight ready. A series of slow waves of the beam were all that were needed to slow the vehicle. There was a squeal from the brakes when it was a few feet away.

As soon as it drew level I wrenched open the passenger door of the cab and pulled myself up into the stifling warmth.

The driver looked at me strangely. I suppose my appearance was not that of the usual traveller. Covered almost entirely in mud and dripping wet, I must have appeared rather startling to him.

I said, 'Do you speak English?'

He smiled. 'You are Englishman?' The

accent was heavy but understandable. I sighed with relief. 'Yes, I am.'

He engaged a gear and we began to accelerate, the twin beams of the headlights cutting into the night ahead.

I said, 'I have had an accident. Please would you take me to the nearest telephone — it is very urgent.'

'Please, I do not understand 'urgent'.'

'Important — I must get there quickly.'

He nodded understandingly. He was a big, homely man with a friendly square face. I was so grateful to be in the secure, warm cab with this truck driver that I wanted to tell him everything, including how much I appreciated the lift.

I said, 'How far is Groningen?'

But I didn't hear his answer. The car that had been approaching us had seemed to be slowing as it passed. Winding down my window, I leant out to look behind just in time to see it make a violent turn. In a matter of seconds I could see it start to close the gap as it accelerated in pursuit of the truck.

I swore under my breath. The man I had left alive must have seen me stop the truck. They knew where I was.

My friendly driver was puzzled at my curious behaviour.

He said, 'There is something wrong?'

I nodded, trying to think.

'The car behind — she is chasing you, yes?'

I said, 'I am a British agent; behind in that car are Communist spies who will kill me if they stop your truck.' It sounded totally unbelievable.

The smile had gone from his face and I could see him struggling with his thoughts. It was a tall story for a truck driver to swallow.

Seconds later, the car drew alongside, edging forward to push the truck slowly but deliberately towards the side of the road. I pulled the automatic from my pocket.

I said, 'I promise you I am telling the truth — they will kill me if you stop.'

The driver, my large, tough, honest driver, made up his mind quickly. He leant on the powerful horn and swung the nose of his truck towards the car, narrowly avoiding a minor collision.

As I expected, the car swerved away instinctively, not wishing to argue with a vehicle weighing several tons. It was a Citroen — I recalled that I had seen a similar Citroen at the house.

The road was clear, allowing truck and car to use the full width as we raced side by side. A quick glance at the speedometer showed that we were travelling at nearly seventy kilometres per hour now.

The truck driver was concentrating, hard, grim determination written all over his grizzled face.

He said, 'They are too small to push us, eh?'

Then suddenly there was a loud bang from the driver's door and another from the steel roof of the cab. I put up my hand to feel a draught coming through what I knew was a neat nine-millimetre hole.

'They are shooting at us,' I told him, feeling at once less secure.

He said, 'You know my truck she is a tanker.' There was a worried frown on his face.

I remembered the shape from when I had looked out of the window.

'What kind of tanker?' I asked, fearing the worst.

'Gasoline.'

With the big diesel thundering, we flew through the night with enough inflammable petroleum to incinerate a village carried in a thin sheet-metal shell behind us.

I felt utterly helpless. I thought perhaps I might climb across the cab and attempt a shot at the Citroen through the driver's window, although a manoeuvre like that would not help my friend guide his giant truck at the speed at which we were now travelling.

There was another bang, followed by another, and then another. The big man by my side gave a short grunt and slumped in his seat, hands off the wheel.

Grabbing it with my left hand, I tried hurriedly to pull myself across the cab to gain control of the wildly swerving tanker. More bullets burst through the side of the cab, some of them screaming in violent ricochets across to the far door.

Then the long, sickening, howling slide began. For what seemed to be an extraordinary length of time the petrol tanker curved across the width of the road with the tyres shrieking in a prelude to hell.

Before it jack-knifed I remember thinking that this was a miserable way to go — and then there was an enormous crash, a tearing of shearing metal, and the fastest growing ball of flame that I had ever seen enveloped everything. As it mushroomed, I heard the whoosh of the ignition. A giant heated cushion pushed down on me — an orange and yellow cushion of brilliant flame forcing me and everything away, away and away.

11

Everywhere the soft, cloying mud. Icy, bone-chilling mud. Invisible fingers clutching at my limbs, drawing the precious warmth from my body. My nostrils were filled with it and I could taste the sourness of the slimy grit in my mouth.

I would have to roll over on to my side or my back before I sank further. A feeling of faint surprise accompanied the slight twitch of my right arm, but nothing else happened. I remained face downwards.

Cautiously, one at a time, I attempted to move my legs and then each arm. The effect was not dramatic. Either I was frozen to the point where I was unable to co-ordinate my movements or I was partially paralysed.

Still lying in the mud, I began to recall the accident. I was alive — not burnt to a heap of black carbon and not smeared in a bloody streak across the face of the highway. Miraculously, I had somehow escaped death from the tumbling, flaming petrol tanker, but where was I now?

I became more conscious of the cold. It was making my entire form almost completely numb. The good thermal conductivity of the wet mud was leaching my life a way. It was essential for me to move.

Then the pain began. Firstly across my chest, inside my chest and clear through to my back. My knees were twin pools of agony sending spears of pain up into my waist, whilst far away the ends of my toes were being compressed between blocks of ice.

Around my lips and chin there was a trace of warmth accompanied by a faint salty stickiness. My face was pressed into a pool of my own blood.

Slowly I began to count inside my head. When I reached ten I was going to roll over. At nine I pushed my fingers into the mud and climbed on to all fours instead. My knees couldn't stand the pressure, forcing me to half-turn and half-fall over sideways so that I was almost sitting, the palms of my hands still on the ground.

I could sense no relief from the cold, but my head was clearing now. Somehow or other I must have been thrown clear, to land here on my face, injuring those parts of my person that had absorbed the violent shock of the fall.

Seeming at first to be in the distance, I could see flames. In the roadside ditch, fifty or sixty yards further up the road, the tanker had come to rest. Illuminated by the billowing but diminishing flames, I could see people and cars outlined in the glare.

Sitting up, I could feel the heat from the blaze, despite the freshening breeze that was curling the tips of the higher flames away towards Hoogaveen. I wondered about the driver.

This time I was free from pursuit. Any witness to the accident would know, beyond all doubt, that I had been cremated. Providing I was not injured too severely, there was certainly hope now, although I thought that I must surely have failed in my attempt to warn Angela.

My watch was broken so badly that I couldn't see at what time it had stopped, my flashlight was gone and so was the automatic.

It was important to move away from here — or was I too broken beyond repair? The cold was concealing much of the pain, I was sure. My legs could easily be fractured and perhaps ribs as well. But I had to move.

Fighting the dizziness, I collected myself and stood up, wobbling slightly. My legs appeared to support my weight, the pain in each knee increasing only slightly as I shifted the load from one to the other. I could walk, too.

Painfully, and extremely slowly, I began to stagger away from the burning tanker, my mind telling me that there had been a house on the west side of the road just before the tanker had begun its sideways slide.

Although an honest farmer could be expected to be in his bed by now, the noise of the accident would surely have woken everyone within a radius of half a mile. It was without surprise, therefore, but with intense relief, that I saw a dull yellow gleam of a light only a few hundred yards ahead through a row of trees.

The increasing warmth in my body was causing a proportional increase in pain now, but I was walking more purposefully and I was almost certain that I was nothing more than one huge bruise with savagely grazed toes, knees and chest. My face didn't hurt too badly, but the blood, which was still trickling down my chin, would undoubtedly make me look rather grim to anyone who might open a door in answer to my knock.

I was almost back on my knees by the time I was standing unsteadily on the doorstep. An old-fashioned bell-pull caused a resonant note to echo through the house.

Steps across a wooden floor preceded the cautious opening of the door.

Somewhat stupidly, not knowing what else to say, I said, 'Please let me in. I have had a serious accident.'

An elderly woman with grey hair stood

staring at me, obviously quite terrified at my appearance. Without trying, I wobbled dangerously on my feet, having to reach out and steady myself on the door frame.

She opened the door wide, allowing the light from inside to illuminate my mud and blood-stained form. A hand flew to her mouth to stifle a gasp. Then she moved towards me, helping me into the warm hallway.

'Mijn hemel! Wat is er met U gebeurd? Wat ziet U er uit! Heeft U zich erg bezeerd?'

Weakly I shook my head. 'I can't speak Dutch,' I muttered. 'I must sit down.'

'Wat? Wat segt U? Ik versta er niets van.'

'I am English — I can't understand.'

Perplexed, she shook her head as she led me to a large kitchen where, pulling a chair out from the table, she indicated that I should sit down.

She held up one finger. 'Wacht even. Ik zal even mijn zoon erbij roepen.'

I sat at the wooden table, numb with pain as more warmth returned to my injured limbs one at a time. A small pool of blood formed from the drips from my nose and mouth.

Almost immediately a stocky man entered the room. He wore a serious expression on his brown face.

He said, 'I speak a little English — I have learned her from the television. You speak English, yes?'

I said, 'Thank God for that — I need your help very badly.'

'You are from the tanker that has crashed — my father he is there already — my mother she tell me you are half-killed and in the kitchen bleeding.'

The woman re-entered the room carrying a bowl of hot water balanced upon what I guessed would be the family first-aid kit. I let her bathe my face, watching the water turn red with each gentle swab that she wrung out.

Her son brought me a glass of milky coloured liquid.

'Please to drink — it is aspirin and water.'

I thanked him. 'It is important for me to telephone to England,' I said.

He raised his blond eyebrows. 'England?

That is not possible.'

With difficulty I fumbled in my sodden trouser pocket, managing to withdraw a handful of soggy pound notes which I placed on the table.

I said, 'It is most important. Please help me — please.'

He pushed the notes away. 'You must do it now?'

'Yes, I must.'

'What is the number, please?'

'Bristol 634972.'

Looking very puzzled, he moved across the kitchen towards a wall-mounted telephone set in a small alcove. He spoke rapidly in Dutch into the receiver, then replaced it before returning to help his mother with her cleaning of my wounds.

My knees protruded through holes in my trousers. The flesh was lacerated and bloody. I was wearing no shoes — they must have been wrenched off in the crash. My muddy socks were soaked in blood and there were pink footsteps across the polished wooden floor.

The phone rang. Bringing the wet chair with him, the young man helped me to the alcove. He spoke briefly in Dutch before handing the instrument to me.

'Angela?' I said, frightened that it would not be.

A man's voice answered. My heart sank.

I said, 'I want to speak to Mrs Angela Brendon,' thinking perhaps I could be talking to the exchange.

'One moment,' and then seconds later I heard her. She was all right — I almost cried with relief. My wife was alive.

'Angela,' I said. 'Oh, Angie, it's me, Richard.'

There was a short silence, then uncertainly she queried, 'Richard?'

'Darling — it's me — are you okay?'

'Is it really you?'

'It is — but only just.'

Understandably, she sounded dreadfully strained, but no more than I had expected her to be.

The shock of hearing my voice after all this time must be considerable.

She said, 'Where are you, Richard?' Her voice was shaking slightly.

'Holland — on my way home.'

Silence again.

I said, 'I'm coming home, Angela, but you must get the kids out of the house right now, and yourself too — you are in dreadful danger — I can't explain on the telephone — just go somewhere safe and not obvious and go at once, then — '

She interrupted, 'Oh, God, Richard, what's going on — why are you coming back?'

Pain was racking my body. I put a hand to my forehead to think.

'What do you mean?' I asked, confused.

Her voice was desperate now — something was wrong. She said, 'Richard, you can't come back.'

'What?'

'Defection to Russia isn't something you can give up, is it?'

'Angela — Angela, I didn't defect — you know that.'

There was more silence. I shouted into the receiver, 'Angela!'

The man's voice answered me. 'Richard, is that really you?'

'Who the hell are you?' I tried to calm my voice.

'Richard, this is Charles — Charles

Reed. What the hell are you playing at?'

Quietly, the first inkling of what I was up against filtering into my pounding head, I said, 'Charles — am I supposed to have gone over?'

'Angela got a letter from you, saying you had chosen to work for the other side, and the Ministry have made an official announcement — the press has confirmed that you defected in late August.'

Holding on to my chair with one hand and squeezing the receiver with the other, I groped for words, a sinking feeling overriding the pain.

'Charles — for God's sake, listen — there may not be much time. Firstly, it's not true — the whole thing is an awful lie. I have escaped and I am in lousy shape. You must get Angela and the kids out of the house right away; there may only be minutes. They've been using my family as a lever, and none of them will be safe until I get back with the truth.'

He answered at once. 'I'll do that, of course. But what about you?'

'I suppose I'd better go directly to the

British Embassy.'

'You've got a lot of explaining to do, Richard. I shouldn't go anywhere else.'

Wearily I said, 'You have no idea what I have to explain. Now please get my family out of there — I'll see you in a few days. And tell Angela I did not defect and that I love her.'

'Do you want to speak to her again?'

'Charles, there isn't time. Go — for Christ's sake, go.'

'Okay, Richard. Goodbye, then — and good luck.'

'Goodbye.'

I passed the receiver to the Dutchman, who was looking at me incredulously.

'You are a spy?' he asked.

'No, I'm not. Could you please do me one more favour before I pass out? Phone the British Embassy in Groningen or Amsterdam — I must speak to them, too.'

He turned to speak with his mother. For several minutes they talked earnestly. Then he sat at the table with the phone book whilst the old lady continued washing my injuries. She was using disinfectant now, but I had more to worry about than the biting pain.

Bessinger had successfully convinced the British authorities that I had defected to Russia. The theft of the PN49 tapes would have made my defection very plausible, and he had carefully rewritten my letter to Angela. He was a clever bastard. I would have a hard road ahead to clear myself, even though I could direct an investigating team straight to the house in Hoogaveen.

The young man was busy with the telephone again. After a brief discussion with someone in Dutch, I heard him say, 'Yes, I will bring him over now.' He passed me the receiver.

I said, 'Hello — is that the British Embassy?'

A very English voice said that it was.

I said, 'My name is Richard Brendon — I am a British subject — probably wanted for offences under the Official Secrets Act. I am at present rather badly injured and request assistance from the Embassy.'

'Ah, yes — Mr Brendon, your name is known to us. Where are you?' There was no surprise in the voice.

I passed the telephone back to the farmer's son, asking him to explain the address to the Embassy man.

When I spoke next, I was immediately interrupted.

'Mr Brendon — the Embassy will be pleased to send a car for you at once. A taxi would perhaps be better than an official car.'

'Am I speaking to Groningen?' I asked.

'Yes — the car will not be long therefore.'

'I won't be moving from here.'

'We look forward to seeing you shortly, Mr Brendon.'

There was a click and that was the end of that. Angela was safe — I was battle-scarred but alive, and Bessinger was finished.

Better still, believing that I had perished in the accident, the Chinese would be sure that I could be of no further danger to them. With luck it would be possible to net the whole bunch at one swoop.

Gratefully I accepted the cigarette

offered to me by the old lady, thinking that one day I would be able to look back on this violent part of my life and wonder at the incredible series of events that I had been part of during the recent few months.

The younger farmer was still utterly amazed at what he had heard of my conversations on the telephone. Coupled with the fire of the tanker, he must have wondered what on earth he had become mixed up with.

He said hesitantly, 'Is it possible to explain it to me, please?'

I looked at the open, honest face. It was people like this that the Chinese had planned to destroy — ordinary working people caught in the maelstrom of the world race for power. Thank God I had been able to escape.

On her knees, the old lady was tenderly bandaging my legs, having completed her work on my face and chest. Without being able to stop myself, I reached out to place my hand on her shoulder.

She looked up at me, her piercing brown eyes studying my face.

I said, 'I should like to thank both of you — you will never know how important those phone calls were.'

I turned to her son. He was waiting for me to explain.

My attempt at a smile was too painful. I said, 'It would take a very long time to tell you my story, and I think it would be better for you not to know.'

He shook his head. 'You are wanted by your Government — you are a spy, no?'

'No, not exactly. I have been forced to work for another country against my will, but it is over now.'

'What is will?'

'May I have another cigarette, please?' I asked, hoping he would stop asking questions. I wanted to think about the best way to handle the situation at the Embassy and my mind was vague and confused.

He passed me the packet, smiling slightly.

He said, 'You do not need to spill the beans — I understand, eh?'

The smoke helped slightly, making my head spin but reducing the soreness that seemed to be setting the front of my body on fire.

'How far is it to Groningen?' I said.

'It is about 32 kilometres to the village of Assen, then 28 more to Groningen.'

That was 60 kilometres — about an hour's drive at this time of night.

'What is the time?' I asked.

The farmer pointed at a brass clock standing on a shelf behind me. It was nearly midnight.

Angela, Susan and Anne would be clear of the house by now in the care of Charles. The past few months must have been hell for my wife; I could imagine the incessant pestering by reporters and the photographs in the newspapers. God, it must have been dreadful.

I lay my head on my arms, trying to ignore the pain by letting my exhaustion relax the tension that was still inside me. Within seconds I was asleep.

12

Someone was shaking me back to consciousness. Unwillingly, struggling against the mental fatigue that was dragging me back to sleep, I forced myself awake.

The young farmer had his hand on my shoulder. Behind him stood his mother and beside her a stocky man wearing a peaked hat and leather gloves stood staring interestedly at me.

Stiffly and painfully I stood up, steadying myself by gripping the edge of the table.

'I am Richard Brendon,' I said soggily. 'Are you from the British Embassy?'

My eyes were fuzzy and one of them was gummed with sticky blood where the wound on my face had been weeping whilst I had been asleep.

The stocky man stepped forward, reaching inside his jacket to produce a large envelope. A seal lay across the flap requiring me to use both hands to extract the single sheet of thick white paper. The official Embassy letter-head was followed by a brief typewritten message, informing me that I should accompany the bearer to Groningen, where I would receive immediate medical attention if necessary and where the Vice-Consul would be pleased to receive me.

'Do you speak English?' I asked the driver.

'Of course — I do much work for the Embassy.' The voice was gutteral, thickly Dutch, but, as usual, perfectly understandable.

Turning to the young man, I offered him my hand.

I said, 'I cannot find the words to thank you for your kindness. Please tell your mother that I appreciate what you have done very much indeed.'

He shook his head. 'It is nothing — you will be okay now, I will see you again one day perhaps.'

His mother smiled sadly at me as I turned to leave the warm kitchen. She bobbed her head, her brown eyes twinkling in her wrinkled face.

'Goodbye,' I said softly.

Outside, the night was much colder. Even allowing for the fact that I had spent some time in the warmth of the house, I knew that the temperature had dropped well below freezing now.

The initial fierceness of the pain was gone, a stiff numbness taking its place, making progress to the car rather slow. The driver had the rear door open for me well before I reached the Chevrolet taxi. Stiffly I climbed in, trying not to bend my knees too far.

Before closing the door, he peered closely at me. 'You are in much pain?'

'No — I'll be all right — let's go.'

For a moment the headlights showed a gravel driveway leading to the gate, and then we were turning on to the road, travelling north towards the place where two hours ago the tanker had crashed. There were no flames now, no fire tenders, and no people to be seen as we passed by.

'Do you know what happened to the driver?' I asked.

I saw the back of his head shake

slightly. 'I hear there is an accident on the car radio, yes — but there is nothing to say of the driver.'

I said, 'I was in the cab — I'm lucky to be alive.'

'The driver — he get out in time, too, perhaps.'

'I don't know — I hope so.'

In a few minutes the big American car was entering the outskirts of Hoogaveen. The town was quiet, its residents safely in their beds, waiting until morning to discuss the dreadful accident that had happened on their main road to the south.

We turned left in the city centre, then sharp right before the taxi was on the main route to Assen. Warmth from the powerful heater was filtering back, making me feel drowsy again — or was it shock? There was a blanket on the seat beside me which I wrapped snugly around my shoulders. If, in fact, I was in a state of shock, I must keep warm; it was important for me to arrive at the Embassy in full possession of my faculties.

Not only had I been discredited in my

native country so that anything I might say would be regarded with the utmost suspicion, but the authorities in England believed that I was an active Soviet agent responsible for the theft of the PN49 attack tapes. I would have to take care in the presentation of my case to the Embassy. An hysterical exposé of the complex at the private house near Hoogaveen would not be received with much credence, even though I had telephoned to ask for assistance and given myself up.

I wondered if Bessinger would be reprimanded by his masters in Peking for avoiding exposure by the engineer who had been forced to work for them by such a narrow margin. He would be unable to conceal all the evidence of my blood-thirsty work — two of his men were dead, men who might well still have important work to complete before the day of the launch. Bessinger would have received the news of my accident with immense relief, knowing that his organisation was safe again. No doubt he would endeavour to check on the deaths of two people in the fire, but the Embassy could easily provide a suitably false story to be published in the Dutch press in order to guarantee Bessinger's peace of mind. Then, when all the arrangements had been made, at one stroke his entire project would be gathered by the West, to be used no doubt as a political means of extracting promises from the People's Republic. Bessinger and his staff would be imprisoned as espionage agents, whilst the Asian equipment would be microscopically examined by Western experts to see if any secrets could be extracted from it. There would be no public statement about the true purpose of the Society for World Political Unity — to disclose the facts of the matter would be unwise. For there to be even a suggestion that a Chinese missile site could be located within the Dutch borders would cast serious doubts on the efficiency of the Western security organisations. No public outcry could be permitted, NATO Intelligence was already regarded as inferior to its Soviet equivalent, the highly effective K.G.B., and further examples that could reinforce such a view must be suppressed at all costs.

Only a few people would ever know how close the world had come to total disaster. On this occasion I knew exactly how close. I wondered how many times before men had died and struggled against incredible odds to preserve peace without ordinary people even knowing of their brush with eternity.

There were more lights ahead through the windscreen.

'Is that Assen?' I asked the driver.

'It is half-way to Groningen,' he answered briefly, slowing the car to negotiate a large traffic island bristling with signposts.

We had joined with the main international route from Meppel now, the E35, and there was more traffic, including numerous large trucks that the powerful Chevrolet quickly left behind with effortless ease.

The driver was not talkative and I was busy with my own thoughts, wondering how rigorous my interrogation was going to be when at long last I reached England.

A half an hour later, more street lights announced the approaches to Holland's most northerly town of significance. I was only minutes from the Embassy now.

I touched the driver on the shoulder. 'Do you have a cigarette by any chance?'

Wordlessly he passed me a packet, together with a half-empty book of matches. Unlike the smaller towns, Groningen appeared to be very alive for the late hour. It was ten minutes to two on a small clock tower as the car crossed the Verbindingskanaal, a waterway which I suspected would encircle the town in typical Dutch fashion.

Traversing a cobbled square, the driver turned the shiny nose of the Chevrolet to the left along a wide street signposted Zuiderdiep, reducing speed to thread the big car through the darting Fiats and Dafs that were everywhere, headlights flashing and horns blowing.

The traffic was thinning by the time we turned right on to the Munnekeholm. I could see young people pressed against each other in doorways, keeping each other warm on this clear, frosty night.

A stop at an intersection was followed almost immediately by a sudden turn into a narrow mews running between two high walls. The lurch took me by surprise. Ahead were rows of garbage cans, rubbish, and dark shadows. Something was wrong — dreadfully, horribly wrong.

I wrenched violently at the door handle, but the door remained firmly closed.

Frantically, seized with the awful realisation that this could not be the entrance to the Embassy building, I hammered on the window with my fists.

With another final lurch the car stopped, its headlights flicking off. Close to panic, I waited — my nerves at screaming pitch.

Then the door was opened and hands pulled me roughly into the cold air.

Ineffectually I fought and I think screamed too, partly from the realisation that I had been trapped and partly because of the torture to my already injured body.

Shoeless, my smashed toes were dragged bleeding over the cobbled yards as I kicked, each movement sending hideous stabs of pain from my lacerated and bruised knees.

There were three of them. They carried me without effort, almost ignoring my desperate threshing attempts to break free. I was dragged in a sea of excruciating pain down a flight of concrete steps, along a corridor and through a door. Then I was dropped. I collapsed in agony on to a cold, damp floor like a broken doll.

The door slammed shut and I was quite alone.

13

The china was the finest Delft, the spoon in the blue-and-white saucer undoubtedly real silver, as was the tray, whilst the coffee was the best in all of Holland. I knew it was the best because I had just been told so.

More than anything in the world I wanted the cup of coffee on the polished walnut desk in front of me, but I hesitated, my trembling hand pausing mid-way to it.

The man behind the desk smiled blandly from his Oriental face. 'Please take it, Mr Brendon.'

'May I sit down?' I croaked.

'Of course — I am so sorry.'

With infinite care, using both hands, I lifted the cup and retreated to sit on the upright wooden chair. It felt luxurious.

My host peered at me through thick rimless spectacles, watching as I gulped the drink. When I had finished, a packet of cigarettes was pushed across the desk top.

The room was warm, the temperature combining with the coffee in my stomach to make me so incredibly sleepy that it required an enormous effort to keep my eyes open.

Forcing myself to remain erect on the chair and returning the gaze of the man behind the massive desk, I drew hungrily on the cigarette until my head swam.

'Who are you?' I said.

'My name is Chang Lei, Mr Brendon. I am an importer of Oriental goods, having substantial business interests in Amsterdam and throughout northern Holland.'

'And in your spare time you represent the People's Republic of China?'

'Unofficially, yes.'

'Do you work for Conrad Bessinger?'

'Mr Bessinger is responsible to me, Mr Brendon. I control all of the interests of the People's Republic in the European continent.'

So Mr Lei was the chief, the organiser, the man responsible for the project at the Hoogaveen establishment. He had a round face with flat jowls and would be in his early fifties. There was no feeling of any kind displayed in his eyes. He spoke English with the pronounced lisp that Orientals find hard to avoid, but there was no suggestion of a high tone to his voice — I found it unpleasant to listen to.

The room I sat in was comfortably and tastefully furnished with a variety of traditional Dutch items, including a large and very old bookcase containing what I estimated must be well over two hundred volumes. My bare feet were placed upon a thick pile carpet, which under normal circumstances would have been a pleasant experience. This time the deep wine-coloured pile could not be felt at all and the toes of my left foot were leaking blood, spreading a brown stain for over an inch towards one of the chair legs.

I said, 'I'm spoiling your carpet, Mr Lei.'

He waved a hand idly. 'It is of no consequence. I shall be leaving here in a few weeks, as you know.'

I stubbed out my cigarette. 'Why haven't you killed me?' I asked shortly, my voice having returned to normal with the passage of the coffee down my throat.

'A man of your intellect might perhaps have used the past few days to arrive at the answer to that question.'

'How long have I been here?'

'Two days.'

Two days! It had seemed like two weeks since I had been able to sit on a chair. For the first time since being recaptured I was not shivering and the air was not fetid with the smell of my own excreta. For two days I had been imprisoned in a single room in what I presumed was the basement of this house. During the entire time I had been without food, without water and without toilet facilities. Under such privation, time had dragged, the injuries I had sustained from being thrown clear from the tanker causing me to drift into what seemed to be long periods of unconsciousness.

Then, when I was on the point of abandoning all hope, a servant had been sent to escort me here for this interview with the senior member of the Chinese movement in Europe. A movement whose very existence was almost certainly unknown to anyone in the Western world. Until now there had been no inclination to speculate on the reasons for keeping me alive; indeed, it had seemed that I was to perish alone in the cellar from pure neglect. It appeared that the Chinese had further use for me. I shuddered inwardly, my bravery of two days ago no longer anywhere to be found now that I was so pitifully weak.

Lei passed the cigarettes to me again.

I said, 'You have agents in the British Embassy?'

'In the British Embassy, the American Embassy and, of course, the Soviet Embassy — the Chinese are a very thorough race, Mr Brendon. I think you refer to us as inscrutable — it is an inadequate description.'

'You didn't tell me why I haven't been killed.'

'Before I explain, I am curious about you, Richard Brendon. Bessinger and Salajar were thoroughly convinced that you would not attempt escape. What was it that caused you to decide to sacrifice your family?'

Was he asking me to tell him that I knew they were safe, or was it possible that they had been captured after all?

I said, 'Every man has to do what he thinks is right.'

'And you thought it your duty to warn your Government of the Chinese bid for world domination even if it meant losing those who were precious to you. That was very brave, Mr Brendon, and, if I may say so, extremely foolish.'

'Have you murdered my wife and children?'

'It is unimportant, Mr Brendon. If they are not dead already, they will be in a matter of weeks. In any case, you will never see them again.'

'So you are going to kill me?'

'That is up to you.'

It was no good, I was unable to think clearly. Lack of food and warmth, to say nothing of sleep, had taken their toll over the last forty-eight hours. Mentally stretched to the point where I could not properly judge the seriousness of what I was being told and physically exhausted with the pain from my injuries, I gave up the struggle to behave as though I was in a normal condition.

Slumping in the chair, I said, 'It's no good, Lei, you can stop playing games with me — either fix me up with a doctor so we can talk or kill me now.'

He made no move, still staring impassionately at me through his spectacles.

He said, 'I fear you misunderstand the situation.'

I closed my eyes, feeling sleep seize me almost instantaneously.

A moment later I was screaming in pain, thrashing uncontrollably in the chair.

Lei stood in front of me, the heels of his shiny leather shoes resting squarely over my shattered toes. The stain on the carpet was much larger. He stepped backwards, releasing me from the agony.

'You bastard,' I snarled at him between gasps.

He turned his back and walked away slowly to the other side of the desk.

'You have killed two very well trained

Chinese nationals and caused a great deal of trouble — you will not be treated with consideration — you will do exactly what you are told.' He spoke flatly, his lips compressing at the end of each sentence.

There was a strong temptation to attempt to kill him with my bare hands, but I was as weak as a kitten, and I suspected he was more wary of me than he appeared to be. Lei was no fool and, although older than I, was obviously a strong man. In addition, the three men who had dragged me from the car were probably somewhere in the building.

I said, 'For God's sake, what do you want? You intend to annihilate Russia and Europe — isn't that enough without resorting to petty torture — or do you like it?'

Lei sat down again. He said, 'It is important for you to understand that you are no longer at Hoogaveen. Your expertise is no longer required and you are nothing more to me than a lump of flesh. It is possible to make use of you alive, but it is also possible to make use of you dead. I have not yet decided which would be most advantageous.'

His face was blurring and the room was beginning to spin.

I said, 'If you want to go on talking, help yourself, but I'm going to pass out shortly unless I have something to eat and something to stop the pain.'

He reached out to press a button on the telephone. The manservant who had brought me from the cellar appeared immediately.

Lei spoke to him briefly, gesticulating with his hands and pointing at me.

A few minutes later a large plate of sandwiches was brought to the desk. Also provided were a cup of soup and two large white tablets.

Lei waved expansively at the feast he had ordered. 'Carry on. I wish to complete this interview at one sitting — for me to undertake my job correctly it is necessary for you to understand what I have to say. I shall offer you only this single chance to discuss matters in an intelligent manner. Any further meetings you may have with me will be on a different basis altogether — I doubt if you will recognise me should we meet again here.'

I began to eat the sandwiches, trying vainly to understand what he was saying. What was the offer he was about to make?

He said, 'The tablets are codeine, they will dull the pain.'

The sandwiches were filled with thick slices of meat. I ate them one after another, pausing only momentarily for a gulp of soup. I reserved the final drops of liquid to wash down the tablets.

'May I have another cigarette?' I asked.

'No — you have eaten now — it is time for you to listen and to decide.'

'I can decide more easily with a cigarette.'

His eyes glittered suddenly, for the first time during our meeting he displayed emotion. Why such an innocent remark should have penetrated his defences I could not imagine.

'Brendon,' he said, 'your time in Hoogaveen has unfortunately led you to believe that you are in some way entitled to courtesy — I must correct that impression. To stamp on your feet again would be simple; alternatively, I could arrange for more exquisite pain to be applied at the push of this button' — he motioned with a thick, pudgy hand to a telecom panel on the desk. 'You will not have a cigarette because I do not wish you to.'

I wished I could summon an insolent smile, but I knew I was not capable of it. A plate of sandwiches and two codeine tablets were not enough to counteract the physical weakness that had crept over me during recent days.

I said, 'Whatever you have in mind, I won't do it.'

'Then your family will suffer for your stupidity.'

'You said they were already dead.'

He ignored the comment and then thought better of it.

He said, 'You are resigned to their death one way or another, are you not?'

I was sure that Angela and the girls were safe, a tiny warm knot of elation formed in my chest.

I nodded. 'If I hadn't have come to terms with that I wouldn't have broken out of Hoogaveen — I thought that in itself would probably seal their death warrant.' Lei obviously didn't know I had telephoned England, and he didn't know whether to reuse the old threat or not.

Placing his hands on the desk top, he compressed his lips again.

'Brendon,' he said, 'in one of the drawers in this desk is a statement that has been prepared which I recommend you sign. You may read it in a moment if you wish, but I will tell you what it contains. It is simply a statement giving a brief account of the reasons for your defection to the Soviet Union, including a somewhat hysterical attack on the capitalistic system you have gladly left behind. It declares that you are, and have been, an avowed Communist and that it is your desire to continue your work for the glory of the U.S.S.R. Your signature will allow you to live in comparative comfort in this house for the next few weeks. During that time you will possibly be given the opportunity to consider working for the remainder of your life to further the interests of the People's Republic of China in Canton at the Radar Technical Headquarters. I will have to check with my superiors about that, however. I would like you to sign it now — I will repeat that you have only this single chance.'

For a moment I was unable to understand what possible use such a document could be. On January 22nd, across the northern hemisphere, twenty-four nuclear explosions would unleash the accumulated fury of the atomic weapons held by the major powers. Entire nations of people would be wiped out almost before they knew it. A signed statement by Richard Brendon, confirming his defection to Russia, could be of no significance whatever — surely, in such a plan, one single piece of paper could have no part to play.

Lei had withdrawn a typewritten statement from his desk. 'You will sign?'

I shook my head slowly, the first ideas of what purpose the statement might serve creeping into my befuddled brain.

'I've told you — I won't help you — you can stick your job in Canton, Mr Lei.'

'You know what the statement is required for?'

I thought I did. I said, 'You intend to use it to increase political tension between Russia and the members of the Western Alliance. I imagine you will release copies in several countries early in January to stir things up a little.'

Lei removed his palms from the table, holding them up in mock surprise.

'Very astute, Mr Brendon,' he said, with the merest trace of sarcasm. 'Please sign here.' He slid the paper towards me.

'No.'

I made no move to take the proffered fountain pen. I said, 'I've helped you enough — to hell with you and your lousy yellow countrymen.'

The fountain pen was replaced gently into a black plastic holder. For a moment Chang Lei was silent. The pause was followed by a sigh from the Oriental.

He said, 'The twelve warheads that will explode in Soviet cities will kill many thousands of people, the other twelve destined for the start point of the tapes will cause relatively little damage and bloodshed. The European targets are principally air bases which are, with a few exceptions, situated in areas of low population. Although Russia is expected to react swiftly, as are the NATO countries, there is a remote chance that the early-warning radar system network possessed by both sides could provide time for a few minutes of consultation by the telephone hot lines. Should this happen, it is just conceivable that a full-scale war could be averted. You understand, therefore, that it is essential for us to create maximum distrust prior to our launch. The distribution of your statement would be of value for this purpose, but, Mr Brendon, there is another way.'

I leant forward to take a cigarette — he made no attempt to stop me.

'Why,' I asked patiently, 'why not launch missiles from China and make sure of the job?'

'Because we have no vehicles of sufficient

range capability and more importantly because Europe would quickly establish the country from which the missiles had originated. Retaliation by the Soviets would be immediate and total; they would welcome the excuse.'

'I won't sign it, Lei — tear it up.' I looked him in the eyes.

'That is your last cigarette, Mr Richard Brendon — we will use the other way.'

Inhaling deeply, trying to tell myself I was brave and attempting to convince myself that I was already in pain and that a little more couldn't matter, I said quietly, 'Which is?'

'You will be taken back to the cellar where you will be subjected to treatment which will condition your brain to accept facts which will seem to be perfect truths when you have learned them. When you have been turned into the person that we wish you to be, you will escape, if I may use the term, from East Berlin. Once on the other side of the wall, we can be sure that you will unwittingly present our fabricated story to the Western authorities. What you have to say will be calculated to severely strain relations between the United States and the Soviet Union. Your part is only a tiny piece of the overall plan to create distrust and tension, but the Chinese are excellent at attending to small detail. The time we spend on you, Mr Brendon, will not be wasted.'

I was shuddering inside at the idea of the treatment he had mentioned. For a few seconds I toyed with the idea of buying time by signing the false confession. If I did that there might still be the opportunity to escape once again. But I knew I was wrong. Once Lei had the statement he could still proceed with his conditioning or even kill me — I could not sign, and I would not sign.

I said, 'Go away and play in your rice fields, Lei — the C.I.A. will catch up with you before Christmas and I'll come and wave to you through the wire.'

Without removing his eyes from my face, he offered me the pen again.

It took a good deal of effort, my mouth was too dry from dehydration, fear and cigarette smoke, but I managed it. The

195

globule of saliva hit him squarely on the left cheek.

His fat finger squashed down on the yellow button of the telecom unit. With his other hand he used his handkerchief to clean his face. There was no sign of rage.

'You are a stupid man, Brendon. In a matter of weeks you will no longer be a man. Your mind will snap to become putty in my hands.'

The door opened behind me. The trusted servant waited for me, a familiar Walther held loosely in his hand.

If I were to fight, perhaps they would kill me now — that was the answer I needed. Summoning all my strength for one final burst, I began to rise from the wooden chair.

The butt of the Walther smacked solidly into the side of my head before I had moved two inches. There was time to see Lei nod his head, and then darkness overtook me.

14

With the exception of the light, it was the persistent dampness of the cellar that caused most of the discomfort. Day and night — although I could not tell the difference — the bulb shone brightly from the ceiling until my head was filled with the light and I longed for darkness to rest my burning eyes. Then, when I could stand it no longer, it would be suddenly extinguished, providing immediate wonderful relief. Sometimes it would remain off for what I estimated could be as long as half an hour, but more often the glare would return in only a few minutes. It was impossible to predict when it would happen, or how often it would happen. It was very effective and it was driving me mad.

During the initial days of my imprisonment the effect of more or less continual artificial light was easily bearable. At the end of what I calculated was five days it was unbearable, my pathetic attempts to shield my eyes seeming to provide no relief at all.

In my cell were two wooden stools, one to sit on, the other to support my daily food tray. The only other item of furniture was the necessary bucket which stood in the corner of the concrete room; it was emptied infrequently.

On each hip and on the point of each shoulder blade I had open sores now, the result of my periods of rest upon the unyielding, cold, damp floor. Sleep was a word that no longer applied to any part of my existence. Occasionally my mind would become quite blank, a merciful void incapable of thought and unable to sense the areas of dull pain that covered my body. In these too infrequent periods of unconsciousness I would remain motionless on the floor, my flesh becoming raw where it made contact with the rough, wet concrete. More often I would lie down painfully on my back with an arm across my eyes to try to force sleep upon myself. Very rarely would this exercise meet with success.

Using natural bodily functions as a guide, I recorded time by a series of marks made on the wall with a plastic spoon. I suspected a large margin of error to arise from my method as my digestive system was becoming slowly more sluggish in the absence of exercise and from lack of proper food. If there had been a window, my suffering could have been materially reduced — just to know whether or not it was daytime would have been marvellous.

The will to survive steadily decreased, as I knew it would. Knowing that I was to be used to assist the Chinese made it difficult to even want to live. If I were to die, in a small way I would make it more difficult for them, although even my lifeless body, left in the right place, could still be used to help their cause. The need to remain alive was eighty per cent animal instinct and twenty per cent vain hope that I might escape in time. As I added more marks to the wall so my hopes of escape dwindled; it was irrational to believe I could ever leave this room.

For the first week I applied myself

industriously to the business of keeping as fit as possible under the circumstances. My day began with a series of exercises calculated to restore circulation to my body after my uncomfortable rest period on the floor. Following this I embarked on a long period of mental activity, when I attempted complicated mathematical problems or strained to remember as much as I could about a particular subject.

For the first few days, my meal tray was slid through a hatch by the door at what I estimated to be mid-day. Then the time began to vary — or was it my own sense of time beginning to play tricks? After four days — Brendon days I called them, to remind me that I was my own clock now — my food could appear at any time at all and I ceased to use its delivery as a time yardstick.

At the end of seven Brendon days I knew that Lei need do nothing more but continue his simple treatment with the light. I was disoriented and had begun to hallucinate badly when attempting to rest. He had plenty of time, his method involved no effort on the part of his staff and it was admirably impersonal.

The arrival of my food tray in the middle of a Brendon night could make me weep in frustration. Internal stress and personal anxiety were steadily increasing, whilst I was becoming subject to what I recalled were termed panic attacks. Deprived of company, conversation, warmth and sleep, I feared the insanity that could follow. The effectiveness of Lei's treatment was not to be doubted. I had read the Compton Report on the Irish interrogations and knew enough of Russian K.G.B. methods to realise that the end was unavoidable.

Added to the privation was the pain from my wounds caused by the escape from the tanker. Toes and knees had turned septic, infected by the conditions in the cell to the point where large pockets of yellow puss formed continuously in three serious cuts. I was lucky that the infection had not yet spread through my weakening body — or would that have accelerated the end, perhaps?

My escape from Hoogaveen had taken place on December 15th. On the wall in front of me this morning were nine coloured streaks made by my blue plastic spoon. Thus, if my reckoning was correct, today was December 24th — Christmas Eve. Fighting down the thoughts of my wife and children, I sat down on one of the stools to squeeze the fluid from my left knee. Gradually, as the pain increased, a familiar cloud began to swirl from the floor surrounding my legs — I knew what is was and knew how to dispel it. Closing my eyes, I shouted at the top of my voice. When I looked next, as usual, it had vanished.

Tears formed in my eyes. It was bitterly cold, causing my swollen feet to appear more blue than usual. I wanted to die — today. Please, God, let me die today.

Unexpectedly, with what seemed to be an earsplitting noise, the door opened. Chang Lei stood in the corridor outside.

'Good morning, Mr Brendon,' he lisped.

So it was morning. Perhaps my timekeeping was working after all — or was this part of the attempt to disorient me?

I squinted at the ugly man. 'What do you want, Lei?' I asked, wiping away the tears.

'Today is the eve of what you call Christmas in your country — I thought it only civil to call in for a brief visit.'

'Okay, you've paid your visit, now go away.' I turned away pointedly. I could feel his eyes on my back. The opportunity to talk made me feel a little better.

He said, 'Is there anything you require?'

'Does it make any difference if there is?'

'No.'

I swung round. 'Then why the hell ask?'

'I am testing your power of resistance, Mr Brendon — you have withstood your imprisonment better than I had anticipated. However, in another week, I think you will be well past the point of coherent thought.'

Just to hear the words made me quake inwardly. I knew he was right — even the idea of another day in this place was enough to make me doubt my resistance.

'From where and when are the drones to be launched, Mr Brendon?' he asked quietly.

Before realising the purpose behind his question, I answered, 'From Hoogaveen on January 22nd.'

Lei turned to leave — I was furious at myself for demonstrating so ably that I had retained the information that I was being programmed to ultimately forget. The visit was over; he had found out what he wanted to know.

When the door had shut again, I stood up and started pacing around my cell, wondering if it would be possible to pretend to lose my faculties before inevitably they would disappear to leave me an imbecile. Lei would be unlikely to set me free in West Berlin unless he was absolutely sure that I had been reduced to an idiot. I could not imagine how he would satisfy himself of this — it was unpleasant to contemplate what method he might employ. Nevertheless, the possibility of gaining my freedom whilst still sane might not be so remote — I would have to think the matter out. I would have to pit my intelligence against Lei's, trying to overcome the overwhelming disadvantage of a weakening physical and mental condition. Perhaps there was still a chance — a tiny glimmer of salvation for Richard Brendon and for my fellow men.

For the remainder of the day I thought furiously, finding that the renewed mental activity was of enormous help, especially in overcoming the feelings of self-pity which on previous days had tended to swamp everything.

It was the first day since I had been imprisoned that I forgot to curse my stupidity for not mentioning at least something of what I knew to Charles Reed when I'd had the opportunity on the telephone.

Spurred on by the knowledge that there could be an answer where previously I had supposed there was none, I resolved to concentrate on this thin ploy to deceive the Chinese. Late on Christmas Eve I was confident that with extreme effort I could withstand the privation, withstand the sensory shock of the light and overcome the panic attacks. At the same time, I would inwardly study the physical manifestations that would result if I let myself go for short periods. Later, under strict control, I would endeavour to create the impression that I had entered a condition of trauma, by exhibiting the physical signs which by then I could be sure would be associated with such a state of mind. To convince Lei that I was sufficiently harmless to release was to become the single aim in my miserable life.

Three days later, the day after Boxing Day, I was much less sure of my ability to carry out the plan. Brendon days seemed to now be of almost infinite duration and I was sure that at last poison from my infected wounds had begun to seep into my bloodstream.

By my calculations it was the evening of December 27th when Chang Lei paid his second call. Mentally I rapidly rehearsed the act that I had so carefully worked out — one slip now and I might remain here for just one day too long so that the thin and precious line of sanity was finally severed for ever.

Crouched on my haunches, I stared at him stupidly from the corner of the room, my suppurating knees protruding through the torn holes of my filthy trousers.

He studied me dispassionately, no trace of sympathy appearing in the slits of his narrow eyes. I remained motionless and silent, waiting for him to speak. Two other men accompanied him this time — probably those who had dragged me from the car on the night of my arrival.

Lei spoke quietly to one of them, but I was unable to hear what was said.

Making my hands tremble violently, which was not difficult, I turned the palms outwards towards the light bulb in the ceiling. Then I brought my head back sharply against the concrete wall behind me with a realistic and sickening thud. The pain was just tolerable.

Moving towards me and stepping to one side to avoid my waste bucket which now was placed in the centre of the room, Lei stooped to look closely into my eyes. He pushed my hands down.

'What is your name, Englishman?' he asked shortly.

'Brendon,' I replied after a suitable pause. I spoke very slowly and with deliberation. 'Richard Brendon.'

'Who?'

'Rich — Richard Brendon.'

'Where are you?'

I stared blankly at the Chinese face.

He repeated the question. 'Where are you, Brendon?'

'Here,' I muttered at length.

'Where is here?'

I closed my eyes, wondering if my performance was being accepted.

'What has happened to you, Brendon?'

I remained silent, but reopened my eyes. He was staring at me thoughtfully now.

I made a low whining noise. 'Turn out the light,' I pleaded.

Lei compressed his lips and turned to leave.

'Please,' I whined.

The door banged shut, leaving me alone once more, but I was sure I had managed to appear closer to the end than was in reality the case.

Ten minutes later I was surprised — even frightened — to hear a tinny voice emerge from the ceiling. It repeated the same message four times, 'Your name is Richard Brendon. In August of 1973 you voluntarily defected to the Soviet Union. The Russians were not satisfied that you were volunteering all that you knew of the PN49 guidance system, and attempted to extract additional information from you by unpleasant means. When these proved unsuccessful, you were released in East Germany and managed to find your way across the wall to the West.'

I listened carefully to the statement, guessing that this was what I had to learn.

About a minute later I heard the hum as the speaker was switched on again. This time I believed I could recognise Lei's voice.

'What is your name?' the speaker demanded.

'Richard Brendon,' I answered hesitantly.

'Did you defect to the Soviet Union in

August of 1973?'

For a moment I tried to think. Then I answered in the affirmative. To my intense surprise, the light in my cell was suddenly extinguished. The blackness was the most wonderful relief. Although I was still allowed brief periods of darkness, these had been less frequent of late and of much shorter duration. I wondered how long it would last this time.

My answer had apparently bought something like ten minutes of blessed darkness. When the light came on again, the recorded message was repeated, to be followed as before by the same questions. Knowing I was portraying a man at the end of his mental tether, this time I answered, 'No.' As I expected, the light remained burning brightly in the cell. It shone all night.

The next morning — or what I thought was the next morning — the system went into operation again. By mid-day I had offered six correct groups of answers and two which were incorrect — just to show that I was largely unable to learn even such simple tricks. Each correct answer was followed by the ten minutes of darkness — it was worth learning the trick and difficult to force myself to deliberately provide the wrong reply.

By the end of the day the questions were becoming increasingly more subtle, requiring a good deal of thought before I was confident to answer some of them. I hoped the delays would be regarded as a result of an inability to remember. The need to exercise my brain was proving a stimulant, I felt almost refreshed in a strange way. Thank God I had hit upon this scheme.

There was no night now, no day, no sense of time. My life was filled with the need to answer the continual stream of questions, allowing only brief snatches of sleep that I was able to win by providing a series of correct replies. Although exhausting, to my sluggish brain it was an exhilarating experience. Had I failed to convince Lei of my readiness for this part of his treatment, there would have been every chance that he would have succeeded in turning me into a trained animal. Instead, because I was playing a game now, I became steadily more alert as I strained to give the impression that I had become an automaton.

'What is the name of your wife?' the voice would demand suddenly. Should I remember that? What was the right answer?

'Angela Brendon,' and out went the light — another correct reply.

Ten minutes later, 'Why did you defect to the Soviet Union?'

This one I'd had before. 'Because of my sympathies with the Communist movement.' I had been taught the answer.

'You are a traitor to your country?'

'Yes.'

'Why?'

'Because I was not prepared to see PN49 go into service.'

'But the Soviets will use it.'

'I was told they would not.'

'You were misled?'

'Yes' — more darkness again; I had been taught well.

Awaking to the blaring speaker and the light, we would begin again.

'Where is Hoogaveen?' This was new

— a loaded question. I remained silent.

'How did you get to Berlin?' I hadn't been given the answer to this one either. I offered a tentative reply — 'I don't know.'

'You are a traitor to the West?'

'Yes.'

And so it went on, hour after hour after hour.

Then, a million questions later, the awful truth dawned on me. It didn't matter whether I had fooled Lei or not when he had come to see me. Sane or insane, this continual question-and-answer game could only have one ending. No matter how hard I thought, or how flacid my brain really was, I would learn the answers until I believed them to be true. All it would take was time. The harder I thought about the answer the more significant it became in my own head, until the very importance of the reply caused me to remember what I was supposed to say. The system was uniquely foolproof and I had realised it too late.

My head was screaming in desperation. I tried to stop myself from answering at all, but I needed the darkness to help me think. So I told them what they wanted to know — it was easy. But the darkness was too short, I had to form another plan — the light and the questions wouldn't leave me alone long enough to switch my powers of concentration to another subject. I must buy more silence and more blackness. Another series of correct answers — even easier to give them now. And then — oh, God, so soon, the speaker and the light. No more — please, no more questions. Answer, then. Only seconds of respite this time — more answers to buy my sanity in the quiet dark — yes, yes, I know the answers to all of the questions — God, how I know them — never ever will I be able to forget the answers.

15

The speaker volume was so high, and I was so near the end when it happened, that the silence came as a shock. My ears were ringing, I was dripping with perspiration, and my eyes were being driven back into their sockets by the light, but there were no more questions — nothing but a gentle hum from the speaker in the ceiling.

Panting, still leaning against the corner of the cell, I unscrewed my eyes and removed my hands from my ears. Saliva was dribbling from the corners of my mouth. I knew if the cross-examination were to start again I would be unable to stand it. The very realisation that at any moment the speaker might once more begin to blare caused me to whimper.

Seconds passed, and then — oh, God — I heard the voice begin.

But it was a different voice, one that I didn't recognise. It was fainter, much fainter, as though the person who was speaking was remote from the microphone. I could not even understand what was being said.

Shouts now, and the sound of furniture being overturned. More shouts, then a series of fierce staccato explosions, the amplified noise making me convulse in agony.

Unable to take any more, my body collapsed and I slid down the wall on to the cold floor. Uncontrollably I began to weep, my battered senses not able to comprehend what was happening.

An hour later they found me.

Crowding into the doorway, four men stared at the pathetic cringing figure that used to be Richard Brendon.

One of them said something unintelligible.

Swallowing in a vain endeavour to moisten my strained vocal chords, I attempted to speak. I was interrupted before I managed to utter a syllable.

'Who are you?'

Automatic reflexes leapt into play. 'Brendon,' I shouted, 'Richard Brendon.'

I squinted expectantly at the light, but it remained on, burning its way steadily into the core of my brain.

'You are English?'

'Yes.'

'What are you doing here?' The large man nearest to me sat on one of the stools in order to reach my level. He appeared harmless — perhaps it was sympathy I could see in his eyes.

I struggled with his question — what answer was required? What was the reply he wanted?

Another man spoke — his English was poor. 'You are Richard Brendon?'

'Yes,' I shouted, 'yes, Brendon.'

He touched the shoulder of the man on the stool, speaking in the language I could not understand.

Gentle hands lifted me from the floor, carrying me from the concrete prison into the wonderful dimness of the corridor outside.

With an arm around the shoulders of these strange men, I was helped, stumbling, along endless passages — all mercifully unlit. I was conscious of

217

travelling in the warmth of a car, occasional flashes of light making me cover my eyes until it became dark again.

When the car stopped I had to walk once more, but not far this time. Then the unspeakable, indescribable caressing softness of the bed, followed by the sharp prick in my arm.

★　★　★

Someone was washing my eyes. The fluid was warm as it ran down my cheeks on to the pillow to form a damp patch beneath my neck. The sensation was not unpleasant. When the swabbing stopped, I cautiously opened each eye to find myself looking at the face of a young woman. She smiled at me, revealing a row of neat white teeth.

'Ah, you are awake. That is good,' she said. Her accent was unfamiliar — not that of a Dutch girl speaking English and certainly not the lisping speech of a Chinese.

I lay in a simple iron-framed bed which was placed against the wall of a plain wood-panelled room. A large window in the wall to my left was heavily curtained and the room was illuminated by a very dim table lamp standing on a low table in the corner.

Another table beside the bed supported a stainlesssteel tray on which several hypodermic syringes had been placed. An antiseptic smell filled the atmosphere — I thought immediately that I must be in hospital.

The girl left the room, giving me another smile before quietly closing the door. Slowly, I became conscious of the bandages and the dressings that seemed to be all over me. Without pain, but becoming gradually aware of physical weakness, I pushed on the bed with my elbows until I was sitting up. I pulled the bedclothes away in order to study my legs. Both feet were swathed in white bandages, as were my knees. A thick pad of cotton wool was taped to each hip and yet another bandage across my chest secured more dressings on to the points of each shoulder blade. I could sense no pain — just an overall weakness, a hollow feeling in my stomach and an awareness that my head was somehow not part of the rest of me. My eyes were sore — any attempt to adjust their focus too quickly causing a dull pounding ache in my forehead. But I could think!

The door opened, admitting the girl. She was followed into the room by a tall man who appeared vaguely familiar to me.

He sat comfortably on the foot of the bed, watching the girl replace the bedclothes over my bandaged legs.

'Velda, she has come to tell me you have awoken, so I have come at once — your eyes they are not sick?' he asked.

'I feel okay, thank you — a little confused and very weak, but my eyes are no more than sore. I'm afraid I don't even know where I am — is this a hospital?'

My visitor had long blond hair cut square at each side of his face. Two long scars on his forehead joined at a point between blue eyes. He was ugly, but not unpleasantly so.

He looked up at the girl. 'There, Velda — you are an excellent nurse, no? Mr

Brendon thinks this is a Dutch hospital.'

The remark did nothing to reassure me, there were the beginnings of doubt stirring in my stomach.

'But this is not a hospital?' I said to him.

Placing a hand upon the bedclothes in a soothing gesture, he said, 'You must remain calm, you are still very sick — no harm will be done to you here.'

My mind appeared to be functioning perfectly, the ordeal of the past weeks had apparently left me mentally unimpaired, and I was able to remember almost everything that had happened. I decided that I would adopt a cautious attitude.

'Where am I?' I asked.

The tall man smiled. 'You will be surprised, I think — you are the guest of the Soviet Embassy in Groningen.' His obvious sincerity at my concern did much to reduce the shock.

At length I said, 'Oh, Christ!' feeling the trembling begin.

'You are frightened, no?'

'Yes.'

'I understand, but it is not necessary.'

It was difficult to believe my misfortune. I had been rescued — or recaptured — by the Russians? What should I do — what could I do now?

The girl placed her hand on my forehead, saying something in what I supposed must be Russian.

I could feel the dull ache in my temples, pounding with each beat of my heart. It was only too obvious that I was not fully recovered and the revelation that I was inside the Russian Embassy had caused a big increase in my tension level.

Inside my head, the pounding was becoming more painful until it was necessary to make a serious effort to calm myself so that I could speak. There were many questions to ask.

I said, 'It was you who rescued me from the cellar?'

The man nodded. 'We arrived in time for you, I think — much longer and you would not be able to remember.'

'You knew about Chang Lei?'

'He was the leader of a strong Chinese espionage cell in Holland. The Chinese have been interfering with us for over two years now.'

I wondered how much the Russians knew and whether they had raided the Chinese headquarters in order to capture me. Even if they had, I doubted if they knew about the establishment at Hoogaveen. And then the thought struck me — a horrifying and terrible nightmare of a thought.

'What is the date?' I breathed. 'For God's sake tell me what the date is.'

The girl Velda answered, 'It is January the eighth — you have been asleep for many days.'

Relief flooded through me — there was enough time left — I had not been unconscious and drugged for weeks as I had feared.

Still sitting at the foot of the bed, the Russian appeared confused.

'The date she is important to you?' he asked.

Through the headache I tried to think of some way of explaining the danger. There was nothing to be gained from telling lies and the time was past when the Soviet Union could be regarded as the enemy.

I said, 'On the 22nd of this month the People's Republic of China will launch a missile attack on Russia and on Western Europe. I know all the details and with help it can be stopped.'

They had obvious trouble in believing what must seem like an hysterical statement from a sick and possibly deluded man.

'You are sure of this?' the Russian asked incredulously.

I nodded, the pressure in my head increasing at an alarming rate now. I would have to rest again soon before I passed out.

My nurse could sense my worsening condition. She spoke hurriedly in Russian and reached for one of the hypodermics.

'No, wait, please,' I said. 'You must listen for a moment. On the twenty-second the Chinese will start a deliberate nuclear war. You must believe me and help me if we are to save both our countries from disaster. I have been forced to work for the Chinese since last

August — there is no doubt that their plan will succeed — they must be stopped.'

The strain was beginning to mount by the second. On one hand I felt almost as though I were a traitor at blurting this out to the Soviets, on the other I knew I had no choice in the matter. I had to convince them.

Standing up, the tall man came closer to me. 'In your sleep,' he said, 'you shouted that you have defected to the Soviet Union; over and over again you have said the same things. We know that it is untrue and we believe you were being programmed to speak these things by Chang Lei. Like us, the Chinese can condition the minds of men, but we do not understand why you were being taught to say these untruths. It is hard for me to believe that the Chinese will start this war as you say.'

By now the girl had become visibly agitated to see her patient deteriorating. She readied the needle, looking at the man for instructions.

I said, 'You must believe me — you

must — I have to tell you more.'

And then another wave of panic seized me. Something in my brain was expanding at a huge rate. Grabbing the sides of the bed, I tried desperately to force myself upright so that I could tell them. Fighting the panic, I clenched my teeth, waiting before I dared speak.

When I felt sufficiently under control to explain, I began slowly.

'Chang Lei . . . '

I was interrupted by the tall man, who had stopped the nurse from applying the needle. 'Chang Lei is dead,' he said.

I rushed on, 'The Chinese have agents in the British Embassy, the American Embassy and in the Soviet Embassy — Chang Lei told me so. In this building is someone who knows that I hold the Chinese secret. Why they haven't tried to kill me already I can't imagine — but you must believe I am in dreadful danger.'

Gasping in pain, I let the girl lower my shoulders back on to the bed. Soaked in perspiration, my chest heaving with the effort of trying to express myself before my head exploded, I tried in vain to relax.

He bent over me, concern showing all over his face. 'I have said you will not be harmed in this Embassy — I promise you this. If you are right about this man, we will find him and we will pull the truth from him. When you are better — and our drugs will help you to become well very quickly — then you will be able to tell us more. Meanwhile you must rest and you must not worry, Mr Brendon — you are safe, you have my word.'

I held out my arm for the needle, knowing I could do nothing more. Seconds later, all the tension drained away, releasing my mind from the awful pressure that was trying to burst my temples asunder.

★ ★ ★

The butt of the small Russian automatic was reassuring in my hand. Beneath the covers on the bed, the slight bulge of the weapon was just discernible. Fully awake, for the second night running, I lay waiting for the man who would come to kill me. To my right, concealed in the cupboard let into the panelled wall, was Niksolk Zhdanov, my tall Russian friend with the curious scars. He, too, was waiting.

It was the evening of January the fourteenth, a bitterly cold evening which had followed on the heels of an equally cold day. In my room were three single-element electric heaters which provided the only source of illumination.

Six days had passed since I had first awoken to find myself in what I had then thought was the doubtful protection of the Soviet Embassy. During that time, my mind had slowly unwound and my body had healed until, three days ago, my nurse had proclaimed that I was ready to help trap the Chinese agent whom I suspected lived in this building.

Zhdanov had listened patiently to my story about the Hoogaveen country house and, in fact, had undertaken some rudimentary checks to verify what I had told him. I had chosen my words with care, avoiding direct reference to PN49 and attempting to conceal many of the details of the attack guidance system. He had agreed at once that it would be necessary for me to be returned to Britain as soon as I was well enough to travel. As a favour, I had promised to assist him in ferreting out the agent that Chang Lei had mentioned to me, although both of us knew that the delay might be inadvisable. To compensate for this, Zhdanov had sent a comprehensive communique to NATO headquarters and to the Ministry of Defence in London.

Both Zhdanov and I believed that our wait for the Chinese spy might be in vain, but for quite different reasons.

The Russians' raid on the headquarters of Chang Lei had been carried out with typical thoroughness. For months, information had been passed out of the Soviet Union to Holland about recent events in Peking. Then, late in 1973, Zhdanov had received an instruction from Moscow requesting him to launch a full-scale investigation into Chinese activity in Europe. Just before Christmas, evidence had been produced that led the Russians directly to the house in Groningen where Chang Lei had controlled the effective Chinese information system.

Eight men had lost their lives when the Soviet party had called on Chang Lei that night, but not one of them had been a Russian. Finding me in the cellar had been something of a surprise, but espionage activity in Europe is full of surprises of that kind, so Zhdanov told me. Along with the eight bodies of the dead Chinese agents, the body of Richard Brendon had also been left behind in the house. Believing that I might be of critical importance, Zhdanov had taken the trouble to substitute a body to take my place. I had not dared ask him the source of his supply.

He told me how the face and hands had been disfigured in order to prevent any positive identification of the body being made, not sparing any detail in his lucid description. Comrade Niksolk Zhdanov was a very dedicated and thorough man, but so was Conrad Bessinger.

The Russians knew nothing of the Hoogaveen enterprise — or had known nothing until they had been able to nurse me back into coherent consciousness.

However, I knew Conrad Bessinger would have wondered if I had talked before I died. Had I, by now his country estate would have been swarming with troops and he, along with the scientists, engineers and the others, would be in a maximum-security jail. After what must have been a period of intense concern, he must have concluded that the missile site at Hoogaveen was safe. Convinced that Chang Lei, his men, and I had been murdered without revealing our secret, Bessinger must have continued with his work wondering if he was really secure or not.

I had argued with Zhdanov for hours about the possibility of my own murder taking place here in the Embassy. If Bessinger genuinely believed me to be dead, then the Chinese agent would have no work to do. Only five people on the Consulate staff knew I was here, the four men who had participated in the raid and the girl Velda. All of the men were considered above suspicion — it was unlikely that any of them would have volunteered to massacre others on their own side. Velda, I discovered, was the niece of Zhdanov and hence an unlikely suspect also. Thus, if I was believed dead, the Soviet traitor could have no reason to become even suspicious.

I tended to believe I was safe because of the clever substitution that had been made for my body; Zhdanov believed I was safe because he could not bring himself to conceive of a Chinese agent operating in the hallowed precincts of the Soviet Embassy. As I had learned, internal security here was incredibly tight; I could well believe that only five people knew of my existence.

To reinforce both our points of view was the fact that no attempt had been made to kill me during my initial eight days here when I had lain helpless under heavy sedation.

By four o'clock in the morning it was almost impossible for me to remain awake any longer and I could hear definite uncomfortable sounds coming from the cupboard.

'Niksolk,' I whispered, 'he's not coming — you're making too much noise, anyway.'

The door opened in the wall and the tall Russian climbed out. He looked very weary and very stiff.

'So,' he said, 'you still believe I have a spy in my Embassy?'

'Yes, I do — but you're going to have to find him yourself later — at nine o'clock this morning you and I have to be at the British Embassy in Amsterdam.'

He slumped down on to the bed, groaning. 'I am tired, Richard — talking to all those Englishmen is not something I look forward to.'

I passed him the automatic. I said, 'We have to put forward a rather unbelievable story; perhaps you should take this in case you're arrested.'

He grinned. 'I have spoken to your Consulate — they already believe a little — it will not be too difficult.'

Whilst the hours ticked by, we smoked cigarettes and talked of my children and of my wife whom I hadn't seen since August.

After finishing the last breakfast I would ever eat in this room, Zhdanov went to collect his luggage, leaving me to dress and say goodbye to Velda; she seemed genuinely sorry to see me leave — mostly, I think, because I was her patient and she felt that I was not really yet fit for discharge.

By seven o'clock we were on our way to the airport.

16

Gerald Longcroft stood up at the head of the long, glass-topped table.

'Gentlemen,' he said, in his sonorous but cultured voice, 'this meeting has not been called in order to discuss strategy, neither will we decide in detail how the operation will be carried out. All such planning will be undertaken by the special groups that will participate under the command of Colonel Corinth.'

On each side of the table, twenty-three men remained quite silent, waiting for Longcroft to deliver what was obviously to be the final address to this morning's meeting. If we were going to be in time, one whisper of our plans could cause Bessinger to bring forward his launch date by just a few days, and the responsibility weighed heavily upon us all. Each busy with his own thoughts, we waited, the cigarette smoke curling up to the high ceiling to form a miniature blanket of smog above our heads. I wondered if the frantic organising had been in vain. Perhaps Bessinger was quietly laughing as he waited.

Three days ago, only three of the men had been known to me. Doctor Derwent from the U.K. Weapons R. and D. Establishment, Colonel Gill of the United States Air Force, and my new colleague from the Soviet Embassy in Groningen, Niksolk Zhdanov. By now, I had been introduced to the other twenty but, despite a sterling effort, I could remember only a handful of their names.

Opposite me, on the other side of the table, sat four of the representatives from the U.S.S.R. — all had complicated names and, so Niksolk had told me, were men of extreme influence and importance. Not that their importance in any way affected Comrade Zhdanov, who appeared to treat everyone with the same rather casual indifference, his attitude to V.I.P.s being totally different to that which he had exhibited to me when we had been alone together in the Consulate in Holland.

I was flanked at the table by British Army officers mixed with a number of serious gentlemen from the War Office — quiet, sombre men who invariably said nothing. Facing Longcroft, at the end of the boardroom, sat Colonel Corinth, a stocky, thick-set officer with a square jaw and a neck like a tree trunk. Corinth was in charge of the ground troops that would launch the attack on the headquarters of the Society for World Political Unity at Hoogaveen. Also under his direct control were the mobile Rapier anti-aircraft missile units which were to be deployed around the country estate. Ghent, Antwerp, Rotterdam and Amsterdam were similarly provided with NATO anti-aircraft ground-launched weapon systems in case one or all of the drones were to be launched from Hoogaveen before — or even perhaps during — the raid. Although the routes that the drones would follow were known to extreme limits of precision, it was believed that some could wander badly off course and naturally no chances of any kind could be taken.

Phantom fighter-bombers, armed with

air-to-air missiles, had already been made ready and were patrolling the entire west coast of Holland as additional insurance. Here in England, each of the air bases from which PN49 would have been flown were being evacuated, whilst an area of twenty miles around each air strip was under study by Civil Defence experts to see if the local population could be moved. Evacuation of civilians on such a scale was an enormous undertaking to contemplate, and it was feared that the mass movement of people, which could not be concealed, might cause the Chinese to launch prematurely when they realised their scheme had been uncovered.

In France, only two air bases had to be protected, the one that I already knew of at Le Creusot and another near Amiens. The French, with the assistance of NATO, were providing defence missile cover, as were the British, although it appeared to me that they were treating the matter in a less serious manner generally.

NATO had, of course, notified Russian

officials of the eastern destinations of all twelve PN49 attack routes. The Soviets seemed to have taken the news calmly enough. From what I had been able to discover from conversations with Zhdanov and with Colonel Corinth, the Russians had reacted swiftly and were at present in the middle of moving huge numbers of defence weapons to areas where drones could be easily intercepted on their predetermined routes. To guard against wandering strays, the Russians had also readied several wings of MIG fighter aircraft armed with air-to-air missiles.

Luckily, the speed of the drones was sufficiently low to make them partially vulnerable to both air-to-air and ground-to-air missiles, providing that radar could find them and secure a lock at such low altitude. There was even a possibility of success using optically guided or infra-red homing missiles. If the precise routes which the drones would follow had been unknown, the problem would have been magnified one hundredfold.

Naturally, everyone hoped — indeed, believed — that the drones would never leave their launch silos. It was Corinth's job to make sure that they did not.

I lit my pipe — a brand new one that Angela had bought for me. Longcroft, the man in overall charge of the entire operation, waved his hand towards me as I puffed out my personal screen of smoke.

He said, 'You have all heard Mr Brendon describe the layout at Hoogaveen and you are all by now fully briefed with regard to the expected performance of the drones should we be unlucky enough to prevent the launch from taking place. Mr Brendon has prepared a drawing of the house which Colonel Corinth has studied in some detail, and further planning for the raid will be carried out this afternoon. If any of you wish to ask Mr Brendon more questions, I would prefer that you do it now so that he will not be interrupted later.'

Silence filled the room. I was sure there was nothing further I could add to the comprehensive statement that had already been issued to everyone.

On January 15th, Zhdanov and I had

arrived at the British Consulate in Amsterdam, to be met under conditions of extreme security by ten officials from NATO, the Soviet Union and from Britain. Niksolk Zhdanov had prepared the ground carefully, tactfully and thoroughly in his earlier communications. After intense questioning, we had been escorted under heavy guard to London, where for three days I had been interrogated to the point where I had begun to wonder if I might suffer a minor relapse.

Soon after we had reached London, the desperate attempts of both Zhdanov and I to present a clear and urgent disclosure of what was happening in the Dutch village of Hoogaveen began to pay off. By mid-day both Russia and Western Europe had been placed on a red alert whilst military and civilian officials had started to pray that we could act in time to prevent destruction of many areas in the northern hemisphere. Soviet, American, British and European leaders immediately took steps to guarantee the safety of their offensive weapon systems. Bessinger could launch his twenty-four nuclear warheads, but no longer could the major powers be deceived into thinking each other had attacked. World disaster was no longer possible, but twenty-four atomic devices exploding in the U.S.S.R. and in Western Europe could cause untold damage and suffering. Bessinger had to be stopped.

From the time I had left Groningen with Zhdanov to the time I had been transported here to the Ministry of Defence, my movements had been kept totally secret. Not only were we aware that British, American and Russian Embassies had Chinese agents operating within them in Holland, but it was reasonable to suppose that their espionage network extended a good deal further.

It was because of the necessary security measures that Angela had not been allowed to see me until earlier today, the 18th of January.

My emotions at seeing my wife again were beyond description. After months of separation, during which I had been consumed with fear for her life, just to touch her again and hold her close to me was a marvellous experience that I shall never forget.

She came alone on the first visit. The situation had been made clear to her as soon as I had arrived in Britain. I suppose it must have been one more shock to be added to the hell she had lived for the past five months. She cried a lot despite my attempts to calm her.

Apparently, our children Susan and Anne had taken the disappearance of their father in a more straight-forward and philosophical way. Of course, they had not been told the truth, Angela wisely only mentioning that I was overseas on an extended business visit. The story was entirely believable and acceptable to the two little girls.

After Angela and I had talked to each other for a long time, she went and fetched them. They were delighted to see me back, noticing at once that I was thinner and that my cheeks were slightly hollow. They were also a little confused about having to remain in this building

243

with their mother for the next few days.

Gerald Longcroft was speaking again, interrupting my thoughts.

'In New York, the U.N. delegation from the Soviet Union is behaving precisely as the Chinese had wished. The United States are taking the brunt of the attack and are deliberately countering in order to create maximum disharmony. I must say that the Chinese plan to cause severe friction between East and West has been very successful. It is extremely fortunate that we now know that the situation has been contrived. Today, it is expected that affairs between representatives of Britain and the Soviet Union will reach an unprecedented level of hostility. Britain has been instructed to walk out of the discussions today, leaving France, West Germany and Canada to side with the United States against the heavily biased Russian opinions on the current political and strategic situation. It is our belief that these joint efforts in New York will convince the Chinese that we are already alarmed at the deteriorating world scene. If we are successful in this, we believe there is every chance that the drones will not be launched before schedule, thus giving all of us time to make the necessary arrangements for the attack in Holland.'

The Russian contingent at the table were smiling slightly, as if faintly amused at the act that was being so carefully staged at the United Nations headquarters. I thought that for once the U.N. was actually being useful.

Listening to Longcroft sum up caused me to realise what a very competent man he must be. I had become a little bored by all the talking that had been done, but as the senior official from the Ministry of Defence went briefly through the long list of complex arrangements that had been already partly actioned, I started to appreciate what an enormous international undertaking this really was. Perhaps for the first time, Russia and the West had been forced to unite, if only for a few days, so that, come what may, total nuclear war between the mighty powers would be made impossible.

Three speakers had touched on the

narrowness of margin by which war had been avoided on this occasion — although perhaps Bessinger had his finger on the button right now.

No one had patted me on the back since my return. I had been thanked for trying so hard and told in as many words that I could have done better if I had tried harder. When I had told Zhdanov this, he had laughed, saying that it was not only the Russians who had cold men in their Ministries after all.

His job complete, Zhdanov would depart today. The ground attack was to be carried out by the British Army, assisted by Dutch military advisers with local knowledge. The Russians had been reluctant to leave the matter in the hands of the West, and had even suggested that an aerial bombing attack on the house in Hoogaveen by Soviet strike aircraft would be the best way of preventing the launch of any drones. Only strong pressure from Britain and Holland had persuaded them that there was risk in their proposal. Bessinger — if he was ready, and I had told everyone that he probably was — could institute launch within seconds of an alarm. The first bomb would have to knock out the launch director — if it didn't, there might not be time for another. In addition, the Dutch were understandably unenthusiastic about the idea of Russian aircraft bombing Hoogaveen, even though low-level bombing accuracy could be guaranteed within extremely fine limits.

A ground attack with the right equipment provided the chance of capturing some of the Chinese Communists alive, and I think it was this reason that finally allowed the Western representatives at the meeting to win the argument. Many people were concerned at the statements I had made about Chinese infiltration into European Consulates and realised that the capture of staff from Hoogaveen could help purge their Embassies of spies.

I was by no means sure that it would be possible to gain access to the large country house without Bessinger knowing in advance. If the drones were ready and the warheads fitted — as well they could be at a time so close to the official launch date — Bessinger might just obtain sufficient warning to enable him to fire some, if not all, of the vehicles. However, not being an expert in these matters, I refrained from expressing my pessimism, restricting my comments to the presentation of a totally factual description of the wall, the gates and the house itself. People more capable than I would decide on the most effective means of keeping the twenty-four drones safe in their underground launch tubes.

Gerald Longcroft had completed his final address and was in the process of closing the meeting. People were collecting files together and the two military guards had started to unlock the doors at each end of the large conference room.

It was incongruous to see one of the British officials open the cabinet that lined one wall to reveal what would surely be one of the best-stocked liquor stores in the whole of London.

Zhdanov dug me in the ribs with his elbow. There was a sarcastic smile on his lips. 'Would it not be better to wait until it is all over?' he said. 'There is still much to be done.'

I thought he was right. I said, 'It's the typical British confidence — they know they will succeed and, if they don't, they will have enjoyed their drink today. We are a practical people, Niksolk.'

'And you, Richard — you are equally confident?'

'I don't know, but I'm going to have a drink anyway — come on.'

Zhdanov seemed to know many of the people who were milling about. He mixed freely with Russian, Dutch and German officials, introducing me all over again to people whom I had met before. My reputation as an international spy was assured. Zhdanov took delight in exaggerating the more violent events that had taken place during the time that I had been loose in the cold, wet fields of Hoogaveen. He made no mention of the fact that I had been kidnapped by the Chinese, although everyone had been told of my earlier misfortunes. My Russian friend ignored all rank, treating Russian and American brass as though they were schoolboys. Only when we were talking together would he revert to the Zhdanov that I knew, a sensitive, sincere man whom I had come to admire. I very much regretted the fact that he would be leaving so soon.

After half an hour of drinking I asked him if he would come and meet Angela.

The Brendon family — which included me — were at present domiciled in one of two complete suites in the Ministry of Defence building. We had two bedrooms, our own bathroom and a roomy lounge in which we also ate our meals. I longed to return to my own home in Chipping Sodbury, having had more than enough of country houses, cells with no windows and Consulate rooms, but I had not long to wait for my freedom now.

Angela had her arms round my neck smothering me with kisses before she realised that Zhdanov was standing behind me.

'Oh,' she laughed, 'I'm so sorry. I thought Richard was by himself.'

I introduced the Russian. He shook

hands solemnly with my wife, who I could see was unsure of him.

'Angela,' I said, 'you know I told you of the man in the Russian Embassy who rescued me from the Chinese in Groningen.'

She nodded. 'The man with the scars on his head.' She looked at Zhdanov. 'This is him?'

'He is my friend and he likes his coffee black.'

Reassured, she smiled at the tall Russian with the blond hair. 'Richard has told me a lot about you, Mr Zhdanov — I should like to thank you for saving my husband.'

He nodded gravely. 'My name is Niksolk — Richard is my friend, so you are my friend — you will please to call me Niksolk.'

'And you like your coffee black, Niksolk?'

'Please.'

With a swirl of her skirt, Angela went to the side-board where there was an electric jug and a small refrigerated compartment containing some milk and a few cans of beer.

'Where are the kids?' I asked her.

'In their room with instructions to stay there — I've already had enough of them cooped up here.'

Zhdanov sat down in one of the armchairs.

'Richard,' he said, 'you have not told your wife about tomorrow?'

Angela turned round. 'What about tomorrow?' Her face was serious.

I said, 'I'm going with Corinth — I have to — I can show them where the important rooms are. I have to go, Angela.'

'Oh, Richard, no — no, you can't — not now. I want you here. Mr Zhdanov — Niksolk, please make him stay.' Angela was going to cry again.

I went to her to explain, but the damn phone rang. It was central control to say that I was wanted for briefing in Room 38 in half an hour. The interruption helped the situation a little. Biting her lip, my wife busied herself with the coffee, realising, I think, that there was nothing she could say which could prevent me from leaving her again to fly to Holland tomorrow.

I said, 'Charles Reed has promised to

come here for the day. He'll drive you and the girls home as soon as it's all over. I'll be back on the 21st — back home properly, I mean.'

Susan and Anne burst through the bedroom door, only to stand embarrassed at the sight of the visitor. Angela introduced them and the atmosphere in the room improved with their laughter as they spoke excitedly to the tall Russian, asking him a continual stream of questions.

All too soon it was time for me to leave for the meeting. I said goodbye to Zhdanov. I would never see him again.

17

January the nineteenth, nineteen hundred and seventy-four. A cold, keen winter's day with the sky a dirty grey and the wind blowing in sudden gusts. In England, in France and in the mighty Union of the Soviet Socialist Republic, twenty-four cities awoke to the chill morning, not knowing that the threat of total extinction hung over them, poised to blast life from their streets and buildings. People rose from their beds to go about the hard business of living another day, having no knowledge of the deadly game that was to be played this morning in the quiet village of Hoogaveen in northern Holland.

Had they known that fast pulse-jet missiles armed with nuclear warheads were ready to carry death to the places where they lived and worked, it is unlikely that there would be widespread panic. With the exception of a few thousand Japanese men and women, few people can conceive the horror of an atomic explosion. Twentieth-century Europe in its seventh decade has grown accustomed to living under the threat of nuclear war, and those of us who think about the matter at all any more, quickly reject the concept in order that we may lead ordinary lives. It is impossible to regulate or live a life by planning for tomorrow's extinction of the species.

From Hoogaveen, two days from now, twenty-four atomic warheads would leave their sterile wombs in the frozen ground to be guided at very low altitude across the face of Europe until it was time for raw nuclear material to unite and radiate in a flower of violent uncontrollable energy. Obsolete Russian drones would carry the warheads, guided along a path that had been so carefully mapped by the Americans with their clever and expensive satellites, whilst the control system had been commissioned by Richard Brendon — sometime British engineer.

I pulled the collar of the fur-lined parka tighter round my neck, wondering if I could have sabotaged the whole project when I had been imprisoned at the country house. It was a futile thought. Behind us, the R.A.F. aircraft that had delivered us so effortlessly to Groningen were departing to fly back to England. The little terminal building was empty but for a few Dutch police who were standing stiffly to attention as the stocky Colonel marched across the flight apron.

Not since the Second World War had so many fighting men converged on Groningen, and perhaps never in the long and eventful history of the old town had such an important undertaking been launched. Of course, we were a long way from the town itself which, under the circumstances, was most advantageous. Such a large number of men could not fail to raise suspicion in ordinary people, and even at this stage it was important to preserve security. The efficient machine of the Chinese espionage network would have its narrow eyes wide open, and Bessinger by now would have become cautious in the extreme.

Corinth was beckoning to me and shouting. I walked briskly to meet him.

'This is Andre Dykstra,' he said. 'He will be responsible for transporting each group to their correct positions. We have twenty cars which have already been packed with the equipment sent out yesterday.'

I shook hands with Andre Dykstra — a nondescript Dutchman with rimless spectacles. His breath formed a small cloud in the cold air as he summoned the drivers for final briefing.

Corinth spoke to each group leader as they dispersed. Ten minutes later, seventy-six hand-picked men had passed through the door of the terminal.

One by one the cars started, pulling away at half-minute intervals from the car park and empty taxi ranks. Volkswagens, Citroens, Mercedes and many others carried the ground-attack troops south towards our destination.

At Assen, some of the cars would proceed to Meppel, where they would turn east along the minor road through De Wijk and Zuidwolde before coming out on the highway just south of Hoogaveen. Others would take the much longer route after turning off at Assen, travelling slowly through Rolde, Sleen and Coevorden on their way to hide near the perimeter wall of the estate.

Six cars, including the one that carried Colonel Corinth, Dykstra and myself, would use the direct route — the one that I knew — the one that I knew too well.

Half-way to Assen, at the village of Vries, Corinth began using the powerful short-wave radio that had been fitted into each of the cars in the party. With great efficiency he checked the position of all vehicles upon the clipboard-mounted map, also requesting yet another time check from each group leader to within an accuracy of fifteen seconds.

His check complete, he turned in his seat so that he could talk to me.

'Richard,' he said pointedly, 'there is something I must tell you before we reach Hoogaveen and begin.'

I lit the cigarette that Dykstra passed me, wondering what Corinth was going to say. 'What?' I said.

'I think that you realise this is nothing other than a military operation and as such you, as a civilian, are not expected to take part. Although this may come as something of a surprise to you, until now I have not been allowed to tell you the truth about the way the attack will be carried out.'

'Do you mean it's not going to be an over-the-wall-and-at-them attack, after all?' I hoped that Corinth was about to reveal a master plan.

He smiled. 'You didn't approve of the attack proposal?'

'No — it's not safe enough or quick enough.'

'But you said nothing.'

'I am not a military expert — I'm an engineer — or used to be.'

Corinth paused for a moment. 'There's no such thing as a military expert, Richard. If I pull this one off, it will only be because my luck has held for one more time and because I thought it out right.'

I puffed some smoke at him. 'Okay, let's hear it,' I said.

'Back in London, we — and when I say we I mean the NATO countries — tried very hard to convince the Russians that a low-level bombing attack was not the right way to do the job. I don't think they believed us, but they did at least agree to let us handle the thing in our own way. In the complex political situation that exists in western Europe it is important for certain people to feel that they are in control of the destiny of their country and to some extent it is necessary to pander to them.'

'You mean you were told how we had to do it?'

'Not exactly. I was instructed to carry out a ground attack because certain individuals believe that success can only be achieved by such means, but I was also told to keep those twenty-four birds in their holes and use whatever means I like. Confusing, isn't it?'

I said, 'Christ — do the military minds of Europe still work like that?'

'It's not really confusing, although I must admit sometimes I wonder if Whitehall understand that military operations are a little different nowadays. Anyway, I decided early on that there was only one safe way, and I've organised things to suit my own ideas.'

'Which are?' I wanted to know what James Corinth had organised; the lives of many people depended on it.

'German Leopard tanks — thirty-nine-ton main battle tanks with a hundred-and-five-millimetre guns.'

I said, 'Good Lord,' astonished at the idea of firing 105mm. shells at a country house. But it was the answer and I knew instinctively that it was probably the best chance that we would have.

Colonel Corinth was speaking to the driver now. We were through Assen and approaching the small village of Beilen, 16 kilometres from Hoogaveen. My watch said nine-thirty.

Dykstra pulled a Dutch newspaper from his pocket and laid it on my lap. He pointed to a long article taking nearly half of the front page.

'This newspaper is two days old,' he said. 'It announces the beginning of a military training exercise to the north-west of Hoogaveen involving Dutch and German troops. Yesterday many army trucks passed through the area.'

'Isn't it a little obvious?' I asked.

'The military exercise is in progress right now — it is genuine enough.'

'And the men we have with us?' I asked Corinth.

'To mop up — there's a lot of wall, from what you've said — we have to look after it all.'

'With 105mm. guns you don't need me.'

Corinth smiled shortly. 'We are going to stand by this car and talk into this radio. You, Mr Brendon, are going to lay the guns for us.'

★   ★   ★

Nine-fifty-three. Seven minutes to go. Bessinger had already failed in his attempt to start world war three; in seven minutes' time we would know whether or not he had failed in his mission completely.

All the windows of the car were open, dispelling the warm fug that we had generated with the heater and with cigarettes. I was excited, and rather frightened too. With success so close we must not fail now.

Several military vehicles had already passed us travelling in the opposite direction — I hoped the Dutch had not overdone the military manoeuvre arrangements, although if Bessinger was to become suspicious he would have to hurry.

The driver of our car was reducing speed now. From the rather vague recollections of my first trip to the house, I thought we would be about a mile away from the gates.

Corinth was busy all the time on the radio link, snapping out orders with astonishing quickness. All around the estate, cars full of armed men were converging on the missile site waiting for the action to begin in a few minutes' time.

A large army truck approached, causing us to take to the frosty grass verge to allow it to pass. Soldiers waved from the tailgate.

Corinth turned his head over his shoulder. He said, 'We'll park about fifty yards from the gate with the engine running.'

He glanced at his watch. 'In three minutes, two transporters carrying Leopard tanks will approach us. The first of these will stop immediately outside the gateway. As soon as this happens, we move forward and park behind the transporter. The tank commander will slew the turret to your instructions, Richard — all you have to do is to speak over the radio and tell him where the first shells should impact. Penetration of the 105 is pretty remarkable — with any luck we should be able to get some right into the automatic launch director system. With a system of this complexity it should be simple enough to rupture a vital nerve that will ruin the entire launch circuitry.'

Half a minute now. Above the noise of our idling engine I heard the roar of the transporters coming, and then there was the first one rounding the curve of the narrow country road.

It was difficult to believe that the time had finally arrived. The car moved forward. Corinth shouted to me.

'When we stop, you jump out and grab the microphone. Don't mess about if you can't figure out exactly where to drop the shells — a few of these babies will soon fix things even if they're not quite in the right place.' There was a grim smile on his face.

Our car moved on to the verge, the timing exactly right — we were going to pass at precisely the correct position. My heart was pounding against my ribs and my mouth was dry.

Behind the transporter, dwarfed by the tank, the driver jammed on the car brakes. In an instant Corinth was out of the door, handing me the microphone on its long lead of coiled wire. I grabbed it from him, stumbling in my haste to find a gap to see through. A pulsing roar filled my ears — the engine of the Leopard was running, growling in its belly close to my head.

And then, from a point just forward of the tracks, I could see the long driveway stretching away from the gates towards the front door of the house.

Exhaust fumes swirled around me and

I could feel the heat from the tank.

At the top of my voice I yelled into the microphone.

'Fifteen feet to the right of the front door at ground level — five metres, if you prefer it — keep on with them at the same place.'

Servos began to whine as the turret started swinging, increasing its sweep through ninety degrees. The second or two that it took provided enough time for the two guards on the gate to react. One of them struggled to close both of the heavy iron gates, leaving the other to dart into the wooden hut inside the entrance. He reappeared carrying a sub-machine-gun just as the Leopard fired.

The blast was tremendous. My head rocked back on my shoulders and my ears felt as though the drums were shattered. The top of the gates were mangled beyond recognition, forming a twisted frame through which I could see the explosion at the foot of the steps leading to the front door. An enormous cloud of masonry dust billowed from the wall.

To my left, the second transporter

stopped, the tracks on the tank moving at once. Like some monster, the drab olive-coloured beast tipped over the end of the trailer on to the ground and it began to head for the wall, its powerful engines on full throttle.

Figures were running from the house towards us. Ten feet away, the man with the machine-gun opened fire, a hail of bullets screaming off the armoured steel tank to my left.

Another shell screamed away at the same time as a hand grenade arced across the road. The explosions were simultaneous.

More machine-gun fire was spraying along the driveway. I crouched behind the rear wheels of the transporter, knowing that there was a good chance of losing my life from one of the howling ricochets thudding into the ground nearby.

Tank number two had reduced a substantial part of the wall to rubble. Belching fire from its evil steel barrel, it moved forward, unstoppable and bent on destruction. On every side there was the noise of small arms as Corinth's men scaled the perimeter wall. Smoke poured from the gaping hole that the shells had torn in the house.

My own tank, the one I was using as a shield, fired again. This time the reaction caused the tracks nearest to me to slide off the side of the transporter bed. Realising what had happened, the commander engaged gear to drive off the trailer. I narrowly avoided a most unpleasant death, the tracks missing me by inches.

Left with only the wheels of the trailer to hide behind now, I curled into a tight ball, hoping Corinth could stop the Chinese retaliation in the near future. It was tempting to peek, but I was far too frightened until, with a dreadful sinking feeling, I heard the sharp beating of a pulse jet, followed shortly afterwards by another.

Two drones burst out of the smoke with boost rockets flaming violently in a near-vertical climb to clear the trees to the south. With the house in near-total ruin by now, I could not imagine how they could possibly have been launched.

Whether or not they would be able to reach their taped attack routes depended on the degree of automatic programming that the Chinese had incorporated in the system. I had no way of knowing how far the drones might travel.

Both tanks, half-way to the house now, continued to blast shell after shell into the building, whilst heavy machine-guns were being used to send a stream of death into every window.

Engineers, scientists, technicians and administrators — men who wanted China to dominate the world — died horribly, blown to pieces by the high-explosive shells or shredded to mere hunks of flesh by concentrated machine-gun fire.

Eight Rapier missiles streaked from the ground in a classic pursuit manoeuvre, each wavering slightly along their established lines of sight. Four of the high-explosive warheads appeared to detonate simultaneously within a few feet of the lead drone, causing a huge fan of red flame to bloom against the grey sky. Seconds later I heard the blast.

Only one of the remaining Rapier

missiles caught the second drone. Although it was perhaps three-quarters of a mile away and appeared very small, the tiny missile seemed to vanish inside the tail of the fleeing drone. This time there was a beautiful symmetry to the ball of fire. There was no nuclear explosion, no mushroom cloud of expanding gas — the Chinese bid to lead the world had failed totally and utterly.

There was less noise now, but there was so much smoke being blown towards me that it was quite impossible to tell how things were progressing from where I stood.

Ten minutes later I stood up to light my pipe — the one Angela had given me. I thought about Conrad Bessinger, about Major Salajar, and about Professor Djambi, men who had believed that the massacre of innocent people would allow their Chinese masters to rule the world.

It was all over now. There was no need for me to cross the road, the job was finished and I felt mentally detached from the awful violence that had taken place. The nest of snakes — two-headed snakes Salajar had called the drone system — had been destroyed, the occupants exterminated and Europe cleansed of evil that had spawned here in Hoogaveen.

No curiosity urged me to inspect the smoking ruin that I could see through the mangled gates. The nagging fear that I had lived with since last August had finally vanished; I was free again.

My nostrils were smarting from the acrid fumes of high explosive, and suddenly I wanted to be gone from this place so that I could think of my future — the future of my family.

Avoiding the muddy furrows torn by the tracks of the tank, I began to walk slowly along the side of the road, my feet crunching still-frozen leaves where they lay in the shadow of the trees. Inside me something had changed; no longer was I sure where my future lay, my ideals were different now and there was much to think of.

For minutes at a time, throughout the recent months, the fate of Europe had depended on my actions — perhaps the very destiny of man had been changed by something I had done. It was a startling thought.

Four wood pigeons flew noisily from a tree to my right, winging southwards in the grey morning. I watched them until they became mere specks against the sky. For man and for nature there was another chance. This time we had been lucky.

THE END